GRIEVING

for

PIGEONS

MINGLING VOICES

Series editor: Manijeh Mannani

*Give us wholeness, for we are broken. But who are we
asking, and why do we ask?* —Phyllis Webb

Mingling Voices invites the work of writers who challenge boundaries, both literary and cultural. The series issues a reminder that
literature is not obligated to behave in particular ways; rather, it can
defy convention and comfort and demand that readers summon the
courage to explore. At the same time, literary words are not ordinary
words, and the series implicitly raises the question of how literature
can be delineated and delimited. While Mingling Voices welcomes
original work—poems, short stories, and, on occasion, novels—
written in English, it also acknowledges the craft of translators, who
build bridges across the borders of language. Similarly, the series is
interested in cultural crossings, whether through immigration or
travel or through the interweaving of literary traditions themselves.

TWELVE STORIES *of* LAHORE

GRIEVING FOR PIGEONS

ZUBAIR AHMAD
Translated by Anne Murphy

◈ AU PRESS

Translations copyright © 2022 Anne Murphy
Published by AU Press, Athabasca University
1 University Drive, Athabasca, Alberta T9S 3A3
https://doi.org/9781771992817.01

Cover images © kkgas / Stocksy and The Advertising Archives / Alamy
Stock Photo
Cover and interior design by Natalie Olsen, kisscutdesign.com
Printed and bound in Canada

Library and Archives Canada Cataloguing in Publication
Title: Grieving for pigeons : twelve stories of Lahore / Zubair Ahmad ;
translated by Anne Murphy.
Other titles: Kabootar banerey te galian. English
Names: Ahmad, Zubair, author. | Murphy, Anne, 1967– translator.
Identifiers: Canadiana (print) 20220198403 | Canadiana (ebook)
20220198578 | ISBN 9781771992817 (softcover) | ISBN 9781771992824
(PDF) | ISBN 9781771992831 (EPUB)
Subjects: LCGFT: Short stories.
Classification: LCC PK2659.A3358 K3313 2022 | DDC 891.4/2372—DC23

Funds in support of research for the translation were provided by
the Social Sciences and Humanities Research Council of Canada.

We acknowledge the financial support of the Government of Canada
through the Canada Book Fund (CBF) for our publishing activities
and the assistance provided by the Government of Alberta through
the Alberta Media Fund.

For Punjabi

CONTENTS

INTRODUCTION

THE STORIES OF Zubair Ahmad invite us into a world of remembrance. That world is defined by the sights and sounds of Pakistan in the 1970s, yet it is also inescapably entangled with the trauma of the 1947 partition of India and Pakistan, which shattered the Punjab region into two, and with the memories that persist beyond it. The stories move back and forth between the yearnings of a young man for a life still to begin and the recollections of an older man struggling to come to terms with the past and its hold upon him. The constant slippage between past and present reminds us that time knows no boundaries, no lines that divide.

The stories are narrated in intimate terms, in the first person. Perhaps inevitably we wonder, are the narrator and the author one and the same? We cannot tell. There are, in fact, strong parallels between Ahmad's own history and that of the narrator who speaks directly to us in the stories. Yet those parallels are invisible to us, as readers. In another form of slippage, the line between story and autobiography remains blurry and enigmatic. As in a dream, it is not clear how much is real and how much is imagined.

Ahmad was born in Lahore in 1958, the child of Partition refugees from what was now the Indian side of Punjab. After finishing his high school studies, he felt restless, uncertain of the way forward. "A different kind of bird began to fly in me," the narrator tells us in the story "Sweater." That bird led the narrator—and the author—westward, to Italy. Several of the stories, "Dead Man's Float" in particular, recollect the narrator's experiences there, seeking a way to survive without documentation, living on the streets at times, among others who were also rendered as outsiders.

After a year in Italy, Ahmad returned to Lahore, drawn back by memories and the affective hold of the city upon him. There, he studied at the University of the Punjab, completing a master's degree in English literature and subsequently teaching at Islamia College Lahore for several decades. These two westward movements, first to Italy and then into the domain of English literature, suggest the capacious scope of his imagination. Even as his work is deeply embedded in the social and physical landscapes of Lahore and in the experience of the Punjabi community on both sides of the Pakistan-India border, it reaches out to engage in broader literary conversations.

The city of Lahore is a tangible presence in Ahmad's stories: its neighborhoods, its roads, its cafés, its landmarks, its histories. We thread our way through the narrow lanes of the old Anarkali market, thronged with people, we walk down the side of Mall Road, and we are introduced to Gol Bagh, a centrally located park (since renamed Nasir Bagh) and the site of important political protests and rallies. Above all, we return again and again to Krishan Nagar, the neighbourhood of the narrator's (and author's) youth—the old *mohallah*. It is revealed as a place of belonging but also of loss, of transition into adult life and the displacement of the familiar by something no longer recognizable. In much the same way, the city of Lahore emerges across the stories as a palimpsest, with contested layers of meaning overlaid on it by different times and peoples.

The figure of Riaz, who appears in the story "Rain," illustrates the simultaneous multiple readings of the Lahore landscape. Only Riaz, a retired postman, knows the old non-Muslim names for the streets and neighbourhoods of the city that were in use before the Punjab region was partitioned, and people come to him to find places that the Pakistan government has since renamed. Contestations over property ownership also gesture towards the violent disruption of Partition. Such conflicts, recounted in several of the stories, reflect the haphazard way in which refugees took up residence in houses available at the time. Such sites initially provided a safe haven but later became flashpoints for conflict, as competing parties sought to establish rights of occupancy. In this way, the violence of Partition echoes through Lahore's neighbourhoods. With the exception of the final story in this collection, "Wall of Water," Ahmad's stories do not explicitly speak of that time. Yet in their treatment of time, trauma, and memory, they resonate with the lingering effects of Partition—a theme that I have taken up elsewhere (Murphy 2018).

///

THE LEGACY of Partition—the recursion of violence and the sense of alienation that we see in the stories—is acted out alongside ongoing political tumult in Pakistan, particularly protests against the government of General Ayub Khan, who ruled the country from 1958 to 1969. Prominent in a number of the stories is the narrator's developing commitment to the progressive political ideas circulating within the coffee houses and tea stands of the city. "This was a time," he tells us in "The Estranged City," "when so many were caught up in the idea of revolution." In "Pigeons, Ledges, and Streets," we are introduced to a young man immersed in the politics of protest. A vocal supporter of the democratically elected People's Party government led by Zulfikar

Bhutto, he had been imprisoned when that government was overthrown by a military coup in 1977. After his release from prison, his mother sorrowfully sends him to England so that he will be safe until freedom is restored. "How much time would it take for the country to get freedom?" the narrator wonders. "We'd been through all this before."

Underlying the hope that buoys the political aspirations and actions described in the stories is a sense of lost promise, of betrayal. These betrayals are not only political but personal, and they are presented as individual losses, even as they speak forcefully about the pressing problems of the day. We encounter the theme of betrayal again in "Unstory," which tells the tale of the tireless Bali, humbly serving the People's Party—"an unpaid worker who helped other people to gain office." As the narrator reflects, "The People's Party did come to power, but what was there in it for him? He was neither literate nor educated. Though his influence was everywhere, his place was the same." We thus see the promise of social change, as well as its infinite postponement, as possibility repeatedly dissolves into impossibility.

The press of the political is closely intertwined with an active engagement in reading and writing. Just after speaking, in "The Estranged City," of those caught up in the idea of revolution, the narrator comments, "But those who gathered at the YMCA and the tea stalls mostly wanted to be writers. There was an unbridled passion for reading and writing." We see this association of the political and the literary throughout the stories. Waliullah, from "Waliullah Is Lost," has a book-binding shop, and it is a place where people gather to talk politics and share stories. In "Unstory," we hear of the narrator reading books all night long and, in "Pigeons, Ledges, and Streets," of books that "brought me awareness of the idea of sharing wealth for the sake of all, and understanding of the pain of the dispossessed." Reading emerges as a refuge, a place for exploration and growth, and as a kind of journey—a way for the narrator (and perhaps also the author) to reach out from his life to a larger world.

Throughout these stories, the narrator seems to seek out something that is lost. What is lost, however, changes: it could be a home, a neighborhood, or a person. Memory joins these losses in a latticework, in which the disparate points can be illusive and sometimes unexpected. Sometimes, it seems it is memory itself that is lost and the narrator is searching for a past through the stories, which become a way of grasping that past and bringing it forward. Yet the narrator also seeks at times to move away from the past, to put it behind him, much as he drives away from his distant cousin, Munwar, homeless and addicted, at the end of "The Estranged City." One senses, though, that the past is not so easily dismissed.

///

ZUBAIR AHMAD—the pen name of Muhammad Zubair—
writes in Punjabi, in the modified Perso-Arabic script
also used for Urdu, commonly known as the Shahmukhi
script, which is used in the Pakistani Punjab. Like other
members of the Punjabi language movement, he also
publishes versions of his work in Gurmukhi script,
which is used in the Indian Punjab, and in this way
seeks to reach across the border that divides Punjab.
He has published two books of poetry and three collections of short stories, as well as a volume of literary
criticism. The second of his short-story collections,
Kabūtar, banere, te galīāṅ (Pigeons, ledges, and streets),
which appeared in 2013, was a finalist in the 2014 com-
petition for the Dhahan Prize, as was his third, *Pāni di
kandh* (Wall of water), in 2020. The Dhahan Prize was
founded to celebrate literature written in Punjabi, both
in Gurmukhi and Shahmukhi. During his October 2014
visit to Vancouver to receive the Dhahan Prize, Ahmad
was warmly welcomed by Punjabi-language writers in
the area and on several occasions was invited to read his
work and speak to writers' groups. He has also been an
active supporter of the Dhahan Prize within Pakistan,
helping to bring the award to the attention of Pakistan-
based writers and organizers of literary events.

Such activities demonstrate Ahmad's active commitment to the Punjabi-language movement in Pakistan,
along with Punjabi cultural production transnation-
ally. When Punjab was partitioned in 1947 and became
part of two different nation states, its language and

script were partitioned as well. Under colonial rule, the Punjabi language had thrived, despite the absence of formal state support. Indeed, historian Farina Mir (2010) has argued that Punjabi may have retained its vitality precisely because it was marginalized by the colonial government, with its preference for Urdu. This lack of state patronage allowed Punjabi literature to remain rooted in traditional vernacular genres long popular among both writers and audiences, as well as in local social and cultural formations that were largely non-sectarian. Thus, even after Urdu was designated the official language of the British Punjab province in 1854, Punjabi publications, written in either the Gurmukhi or the Shahmukhi script, continued to flourish.

At the time of independence, in 1947, the Punjab was partitioned along sectarian lines, with contiguous Muslim-majority areas allocated to Pakistan and non-Muslim-majority areas to India. The Punjabi language fared differently in the two new countries. In India, plans to redraw internal state boundaries along linguistic lines were delayed in the case of the Punjab region, and activism in support of a Punjabi-language state was widely viewed as a Sikh political project. It was only in 1966, after prolonged agitation, that a Punjabi-speaking state was finally established, while purportedly Hindi-speaking areas were incorporated into the newly created state of Haryana—although it is well known that Hindus were encouraged to list Hindi as their mother tongue on their census returns so as to influence the boundaries of the new state. As this controversy demonstrates, Punjabi, too, was imbricated in divisive politics related to religious identity, in this case involving Sikhs and Hindus.

In Pakistan, however, Urdu prevailed. Punjabi is the language of a significant proportion of the Pakistani population—roughly 40 percent—but Urdu is the official language at the provincial as well as national level. Again, the issue of language proved divisive in the early decades of Pakistan's existence. The effort to impose Urdu in East Pakistan ultimately failed, triggering a conflict that ended with the formation of Bangladesh in 1971. In West Pakistan, however, advocates for Punjabi were active throughout this period and have remained so to this day.

Although, as Julien Columeau (2021) demonstrates, conservative and nationalist positions have been articulated within the larger movement in support of the Punjabi language in Pakistan, the voice of the Left has been particularly prominent. The relationship between the Punjabi-language movement and leftist programs and struggles has drawn the attention of scholars such as Virinder Kalra and Waqas Butt (2013) and Sara Kazmi (2017, 2018). "As the language of the uneducated—of the peasants and working class," Kalra and Butt observe, Punjabi is "shunned by the nationalist elite. Yet it is precisely this status that provides the rationale for its appeal to Left-wing groups and parties" (2013, 539). Support for Punjabi is grounded in a commitment to addressing local and material needs and to restructuring the distribution of wealth in more equitable ways, so as to reduce disparities among social classes. To that end, early childhood education, along with the right of children to receive that education in their mother tongue, rather than in Urdu, has been a major focus of pro-Punjabi activism in Pakistan.

We can see connections to this larger Punjabi-language movement in the social and political commitments that animate the stories here, in which the narrator embraces leftist ideas and activism. But Ahmad's commitment to the Punjabi language in Pakistan is expressed in other ways as well. He has revived a Punjabi-language book shop, Kitab Trinjan, formerly in operation from 1997 to 2009, and he was earlier active in the now-defunct Punjabi-language daily newspaper *Sajjan* ("Friend"), serving as assistant editor on a volunteer basis from 1988 to 1990. He seeks through such endeavours to enhance engagement with the work of Punjabi-language writers, as well as to raise the public profile of Punjabi in Pakistan.

In 2006, Ahmad visited India—a visit that informs his story "Wall of Water" (a story written considerably after the others in this collection). He set out partly to explore his ancestral places, but while he was there, he met with local writers, just as he meets with Indian writers who visit Pakistan—and just as he likewise met with Punjabi-language writers during his visit to Canada. This crossing not only of boundaries but also of cultural contexts is integral to the articulation of a contemporary Punjabi literary domain.

///

AHMAD'S STORIES position the post-colonial state of Pakistan within a framework of loss—the loss of a once-shared culture, of ties to places now out of reach. Yet they speak to the losses of our moment as well, when the neoliberal state and corporate values have prevailed, and our responses to them are constrained by our sheer powerlessness to resist. Perhaps memory is all we have, in the face of the relentless march of the current global economic and political order, in the path of which tens of millions have been forced to flee their homes, many of them now formally stateless. This sense of irretrievable loss—this constant slipping away of what was—accounts for Ahmad's focus on deprivation, his embrace of memories of Lahore prior to Partition and the names that defined it, memories that both consume and evade him.

There is no easy recourse from both the bitterness and the sweetness of the past in Ahmad's stories, no simple release from its hold upon us. Time flows forwards and backwards, as past and present merge in the narrative landscape. Perhaps the temporal flux that permeates his writing stands at the heart of what it means to write in Punjabi at all—to tap into memory that moves beyond separation and asserts itself from within, oblivious to distinctions between here and there, now and then. There is, in other words, something that does continue, something that remains whole. At the same time, the very fact of division—the impossibility of reunion, of erasing the border to form a single nation—imbues Punjabi writing with a peculiar power, freeing it, perhaps, to speak of something else. That something else is something human, something shared, that cannot be confined in a vessel as limiting as a nation.

By situating us in the past within our own present, Ahmad calls us to account for the harsh material and political circumstances of our time, implicitly asking us to confront the same state of division that Punjabis on both sides of the border daily inhabit. He also moves us beyond that physical border to those borders, and border crossings, that reside within ourselves, often floating just beyond the limits of language, in affects and perceptions that defy easy articulation. These broader realms of human experience transcend the intimacies and specificities of any one language, and it is in recognition of this that these stories are presented here in translation. We do so, however, with full acknowledgement of the degree to which their transposition into English leaves Punjabi behind. Punjabi, too, must remain as a memory here, a linguistic landscape in which these stories no longer dwell but that continues to shape them and give them birth.

///

THESE STORIES represent the end product of a profes-
sional friendship of almost a decade. I first met Zubair
Ahmad in 2014. I had been active in helping to establish
the Dhahan Prize for Punjabi Literature in 2013 and had
learned of him and his work in that context. Although
I had travelled to the Indian Punjab many times, I had
never visited the Pakistan side of the border. So while I
was on sabbatical in India in 2013–14, I decided to visit
Lahore, for the very first time.

There is a saying in Punjabi: "Until one has seen
Lahore, one has not been born." This resonated with
me: It seemed to me as if I had been waiting to arrive
there my whole life, without knowing it. Zubair Ahmad
played a pivotal role in that arrival, introducing me to
people and places in that vibrant and beautiful city.
One of the highlights of my week-long stay was my
first visit to Sangat, a weekly poetry gathering at the
home of Najm Hosain Syed, a prominent figure in the
Punjabi-language movement in Pakistan. As Zubair had
promised, this was a magical experience. At Sangat,
attendees gathered in a circle—now, since Covid-19,
it takes place over Zoom, but the general form of
the meeting is the same. A poem is distributed, and
each person in the circle reads the poem in turn. An
in-depth conversation then follows. After a couple of
hours, the poem is sung. Then, in its in-person form, the
group shared *naan* bread and *daal* in a communal meal
known as *langar;* now, over Zoom, participants share
songs and further discussion. In person or over Zoom,

it is a gathering where Punjabi literature truly comes to life.

The idea of translating these stories was born during that first visit in 2014, and the work progressed slowly and almost entirely virtually over the following years. It was a collaborative process. We used Skype, in those days before Zoom, and exchanged emails full of drafts, discussion, and redrafts. No piece of writing is ever really finished, and this seems especially true of translations. There is always one more small refinement to be made, one more way to convey an elusive image or idea. As with all writing, though, a translation reaches a point where it needs to be declared done and cast out into the world. It is in this spirit that we give you these stories, and we hope you enjoy them.

REFERENCES

Columeau, Julien. 2021. "'Urdu Is Punjab's Mother Tongue': The Urdu/ Punjabi Controversy Between 1947 and 1953 in Pakistani Punjab." *SINDHU: Southasian Inter-Disciplinary Humanities* 1, no. 1. https:// sindhuthejournal.org/index.php/sindhuthejournal/article/view/ urdu_is_punjabs_mother_tongue_juliencolumeau.

Kalra, Virinder S., and Waqas M. Butt. 2013. "'In one hand a pen in the other a gun': Punjabi Language Radicalism in Punjab, Pakistan." *South Asian History and Culture* 4, no. 4: 538–53. https://doi.org/10.1080/ 19472498.2013.824682.

Kazmi, Sara. 2017. "The Marxist Punjabi Movement: Language and Literary Radicalism in Pakistan." *Südasien-Chronik / South Asia Chronicle* 7/2017: 227–50. Available at https://edoc.hu-berlin.de/ handle/18452/19500.

———. 2018b. "Of Subalterns and Sammi Trees: Echoes of Ghadar in the Punjabi Literary Movement." *Socialist Studies / Études socialistes* 13, no. 2: 114–33.

Mir, Farina. 2010. *The Social Space of Language: Vernacular Culture in British Colonial Punjab*. Berkeley: University of California Press.

Murphy, Anne. 2018. "Remembering a Lost Presence: The Spectre of Partition in the Stories of Lahore-Based Punjabi-Language Author Zubair Ahmed." In *Partition and the Practice of Memory*, edited by Churnjeet Mahn and Anne Murphy, 231–54. London: Palgrave Macmillan.

GRIEVING *for* PIGEONS

Waliullah Is Lost

IT WAS A dull morning, without a hint of sun. We were on our way to school, shivering with cold and hanging our school bags carefully at our waists, moving as quickly as we could. We bantered back and forth as we passed the shops: there was the sweet seller, the old lady with the ink pots, and the gentleman who sells *sonf*, or anise seed. It was Pheeqa, Kala the black, me, and Waliullah. We were a crew. After everyone gathered for the first prayer, all the boys ran across the big courtyard to their classrooms, in lines. We arrived just in time at the big school gate and ran to catch up with our class. None of the teachers saw us sneak in: there was too much of a ruckus as the boys rushed in after prayers. The teachers gossiped among themselves as usual, too, so they didn't pay us any mind. One had to be careful, though, when rushing in lines like that. If someone pushed someone else out of line from behind, or if someone slow or weak suddenly fell, that child would be beaten. This was our daily routine.

Every day, after entering the class, we ran to our benches. Each of us had our own. In the primary years, we had only a coarse sackcloth to sit on, but there were benches and desks in the higher grades. After we rubbed the cold benches with our school bags to warm them, only one thing came to mind, like a blast of cold air: don't get beaten. Everyone kneaded their hands together and blew on them to keep them warm: the cold was so intense that we could barely hold our pens. In winter, our only desire was not to be beaten in the first or second period. In the intense morning cold, the pain was just too much.

It was time for class with the Urdu teacher, Mr. Altaf. Unlike the rest of us, Mr. Altaf's mother tongue was Urdu. He always wore pure cotton—a long white kurta and pyjama pants—and *makesh*, a kind of boot. He chewed bright red betel leaf in his mouth, was of medium height, and spoke hesitatingly in an ostentatiously cultured and refined way. He was one of the few teachers who didn't carry a stick in his hands, so the boys weren't too afraid of him.

4

But he did have his own special method of punishment. He would call a student to him, very close, and would twist the student's ear so forcefully that the boy would twist and turn in front of him. Mr. Altaf wouldn't move a muscle, nor would he allow the boy to move away. Then he would make jokes about it, addressing the class, "He looks like he is enjoying it, don't you think? He's dancing so well!" The boy would be so close to him that his betel leaf–soaked breath would sprinkle deep red juice on the boy's face. Sometimes, for a change, he would pinch a boy on the abdomen instead and stand steady and tall; the boy would twist around, back and forth, and the class would be doubled over with laughter. Of course, if anyone laughed too loud, he'd be called up to the front as well. While pinching the boy, Mr. Altaf would watch the class closely, chewing his betel leaf, as if he were asking for accolades for his special skill. "Look at how beautifully I do my work," he seemed to say. According to him, his method of punishment was both a pragmatic technique and an art. He had earned this skill after working in schools for many years.

But sometimes something else would happen. Trembling with anger, he would ask a boy to bring a stick from the teacher in the adjacent classroom. This would only happen once a year or so. Punishing with a stick wasn't his thing. So, when he did it, it went all wrong. He would beat his victim blindly, screaming abuses, and there seemed to be no end to it. "You fucker! You motherfucker!" he would yell. The class would become deathly silent. As the student left to bring the stick from the other class, Mr. Altaf would walk among the rows of benches and wherever he would stop, it was as if death itself had struck.

This would happen when someone made a joke that crossed the limits of his patience. It happened, for example, when a new oil to grow hair had appeared in the market. It had become quite famous. It was called "Zaidal," or something like that. That day, because of the cold, no one had the heart to open their school bags or books. After taking attendance, as usual, he asked the students to open their books. That's when someone mentioned the oil. Even though it had been whispered, he had heard it. He was bald. And he became very angry. He asked the boy who was sitting in front of our bench, who was also the class monitor, to bring the stick from the next class.

Suddenly, it was as if someone had forced our hands into ice. Not only our class. It seemed as if the whole school was engulfed in silence. When the boy came with the stick, we sat lifeless, as if we had lost our very souls. We all knew the joke had been made by the son of Phaje the butcher. At the end of eighth grade, he quit school and started working in his father's shop in the bazaar.

Mr. Altaf walked once or twice between the benches and then came and stood near us. Our hands were already numb at even the thought of a beating. When I think of it today, it seems to me that perhaps Waliullah had moved a bit, or that he didn't have the same kind of fear on his face that the rest of us had. It was rare that he would be chosen. But that day our Mr. Altaf asked Waliullah to come out, gesturing with his stick. His face turned red with fury and betel juice seeped from his lips. Waliullah continued to look at him as before. His face was unreadable.

When Mr. Altaf decided to deliver his punishment, there was no question of justice. Whether someone was guilty or not, he would suffer. In reality, Mr. Altaf usually didn't have a clue about who had made mischief. He would just call a boy up to the front of the class, any boy, and beat that boy blindly; anyone he called upon had to put out his hands for the beating. If a boy tried to speak up or say something in his own defence, the beating would be all the more severe.

Mr. Altaf raised his stick and Waliullah put forward his hands. The beating began, and it continued. We sat there, frozen. Some boys from other classes watched stealthily from the door. Waliullah was beaten just past the threshold. Only God knows what happened to Mr. Altaf: he struck with rage, with fury, and at last Waliullah's hands began to hang limply. His eyes filled with tears. But brave Waliullah! He neither wept nor cried out. The stick broke after the hundred-and-second strike. Silence engulfed the school. By recess, everyone knew. "Waliullah has been beaten!" Everyone said his name loudly, stretching it out. He silently left school. His hands were swollen and red, and someone had covered them with a handkerchief. Until he left for home, we blew over his hands, with the handkerchief over them, soothingly. He did not move them.

Waliullah was our friend, our companion, the connecting tissue of our group. He was short in stature and a bit frail. He lagged behind the other boys in class. His nose was long like a parrot's, and on his head he always wore a filthy cap, the kind used by those who perform the *namāz,* or Muslim prayers. He always bowed his head down as he walked, as if something had fallen and he was looking for it; then his nose would look even longer. He was the most gentle and good-hearted among us. He was so weak that he couldn't even play some of our games. When we would play, he would sit near us and act as a judge or take care of our shoes or other things. Whenever some disagreement arose in a game, he was the one to decide what was fair.

The boys from the higher grades also respected him, but not for the reasons we did. He was looked up to because of his ability to call on God's power, chanting Qur'anic verses and then blowing on a person's forehead as a blessing. This was why everyone called him "Waliullah," the friend of God. His real name was something else. A boy would lean his forehead towards him and say, "Waliullah, blow on my forehead." Waliullah would stand very seriously, clasp the boy's forehead gently, and after reciting something under his breath, blow on it. That warm and gentle puff on the forehead seemed to reach deep inside. The boys were so enamoured of this that sometimes they would crowd around

8

him and, one by one, come forward, stepping back only after receiving his special breath. Most of them did it so that with this, perhaps they might be saved from being beaten. Some must have had other wishes, too. There was trust, warmth and comfort in Waliullah's breath.

Now that he had beaten Waliullah so severely, we all were sure Mr. Altaf would not be spared. "How could he have beaten Waliullah?" Then the expected happened. We reached school the next morning and found that it was closed. Mr. Altaf's wife had died. Now everyone repeated Waliullah's name with awe. Instead of going to Mr. Altaf's home to pay condolences, half the school went to Waliullah's home to enquire after his health. Everyone from the school wanted to feel his breath upon them. Even women from the *mohallah* started to seek out his blessing. After that, he was never beaten again. We came to know many years later that Mr. Altaf's wife had tuberculosis, and she had already been very sick for a long time. But that didn't matter.

Waliullah was not only my classmate; he also lived in my *mohallah*. I can't say now how long we had been friends. It seems to me that we always were. After the partition of Punjab in 1947, our fathers used to sit together every evening in Tufail's tailor shop. I remember that there was a large low wooden table, and on one side a sewing machine and an iron that would be warmed by coals: the hookah was prepared from the coals used to heat the iron, or sometimes the hookah's

9

coals were used to prepare the iron. In this way, the two lent each other smoke. Tufail the tailor never measured any of his customers. He would just look at a person carefully, or he might put his hand on the man's or child's shoulder, examine him from head to foot and say, "You can have your clothes day after tomorrow." In the Daultana years, just after Partition, people would gather there in the evening after work for news of Amritsar and Gurdaspur on the Indian side; this continued on through the Ayub regime, Bhashani's leadership in East Pakistan, and then Bhutto's time at the helm. All these politicians and politics came and went. All the black turned grey. Then Tufail's shop was closed, and a medical store opened in its place. Now there is a big bakery there, with huge glass windows.

When school finally finished, we waited for our results. In those days in Lahore, special editions of newspapers were published with the results of the final exams at the end of grade 10, and news hawkers called out loudly to sell copies. When the news finally came, we found out that Waliullah had failed. We felt no joy over how we did or didn't place. We couldn't bear the grief of Waliullah's failure. We sat together in silence on the side of the road, in the centre of the *mohallah*, for a long time. Back then you could hire a bicycle for just a few pennies, four or eight annas, per hour. We were so upset that we hired bicycles and rode like mad all over the city. Cycling frantically, we tired ourselves out, but we still found no peace. It used to be deserted beyond Bund Road, at the edge of the city. There were thick trees and fields. Among them were some wells, the barking of dogs, and the tolling of bells. We went and sat at one of the wells. Pheeqa brought out a packet of Woodbine cigarettes, which he had stolen from his father. We all lit up cigarettes and became exhausted from coughing. But even then, we could not relax. We had no idea that from that time on we would never be relaxed again, that this pain was only the beginning. Some of us went on to university, and one suddenly left for Karachi. Another was sent abroad by his father. Some took care of their fathers' shops, others became bus conductors, and someone joined an office. One or two boys went back to their villages. There were just a few of us left who knew each other from those days. It seemed like the whole world changed.

Waliullah's father had a book-binding shop. What a place it was! Built on a pile of dirt in a corner of one of the narrow lanes in the main market, it was just a kiosk of tin and wood, attached to a small two-story house they lived in. Children's magazines, detective novels, political and other magazines, old and new, all used to hang there as the book-binding work carried on. In the evening, the shop was transformed into a gathering place for people to gossip and discuss politics. When Waliullah's father grew old, his son took charge of the shop. That is how it was supposed to be, so that is how it was. At the same time, Waliullah's sisters needed to be married off, and it seemed to us that Waliullah had become even more frail from the heavy burden he

carried. Then we, too, were forced to leave the *mohallah*.
I never thought it would happen to us, but it did, and
then to Waliullah as well.

I used to visit the old neighbourhood once or twice
every year, and whenever I went, I would visit Waliullah's
shop. He had turned completely grey and was even thin-
ner and smaller. His cap was even muddier than before.
His father was bedridden. One or two sisters had been
married, and one or two, perhaps not. He himself had
gotten married, too, and had children. The old *mohallah*
and marketplace in Lahore had changed. The price of
land had skyrocketed. The bazaar filled with people.
Whenever I used to visit, there were always one or two
new shops—but if one thing remained unchanged, it
was Waliullah's shop. But the building was under dispute. After Partition, as a refugee from the now-Indian
side of Punjab, his father had occupied the upper portion of the house. Someone else took up its lower portion.
The case regarding who was the rightful owner had
been in court ever since. Waliullah was very worried
about it. There were other problems with the shop as
well: things and places that used to be secured through
long-standing personal relationships were being torn
apart under the onslaught of the new cash economy.
When I would sit in his shop, we would talk about the
old days. The place was tiny. Showing me to a stool, he
would call for tea. The tea would be served in a glass,
with a small saucer. He would pour half the tea into
the saucer and give me the glass. Then, it was as if he

opened the book of the *mohallah* to read from, and he would start to talk.

"A year has gone by since Fareeda came home. One day, there she was, with three children. She asked about you, and I said I didn't know where you were. Lali sold his house and moved to Defence, in the new part of town. We heard that they built a big house there. It looks like Lali's father had his hands in a lot of things . . . Kala is still operating a printing press, and he probably always will. Pheeqa opened a hardware shop, and his wife is a schoolteacher. She never leaves him in peace. But then again, he never managed to say much before, anyway. Sukky has given into heroin. Pakaure—he used to love eating those salty snacks!—spent two months in jail after stabbing the son of the goldsmith. Naifey's fish shop is doing very well; he was the oldest in the family. Dullah still hasn't settled down yet. He has left his life of crime behind, but he still has no steady job. He was saying that he might start selling chickens. Aftikar Allahi became a senior officer in a bank." So many things to discuss, to finish up with.

Then time passed, and I hadn't had a chance to visit the old *mohallah* for a long while. Finally, one day when I happened to be in the area, I went to Waliullah's shop. But I couldn't find it. Part of me was not surprised: places in this part of the city change like newly rich relatives. I looked closely and now shoes were being sold where his shop used to be, and another person was sitting in his place. Women and children were standing around, waiting to buy something. There was never such a crowd at Waliullah's shop. I asked the new shopkeeper about what became of Waliullah, but he didn't answer; instead, he got annoyed and said he didn't have time to talk. "Besides," he added, "why are you asking about him?" Inquiring at many shops, I finally reached Bashir Hamam, who ran a *hamām* and barber shop. When the first public protest movement against President Ayub was launched, Bashir was the first in the whole market to hang a photo of Zulfikar Ali Bhutto in his shop. One time, people from the Islamist party came to vandalize his bathhouse, and he had stood alone in front of it, holding a naked razor. No one dared to come near. This made him very famous in the bazaar, so much so that during the first election, when Bhutto visited the area, Bashir posed with him and others for a photo that he displayed in his shop from then on. But now, I saw, Bashir had grown very old. Most of the work was done by boys, and he would just help to bring soap and towels to customers. I asked: "Do you recognize me?" He replied: "Even if you came after one hundred years, I would recognize you. I cut your hair for twenty-three years."

There was a flash in his eyes when I asked about Waliullah. "How long has it been since you last came around? He lost the court case over his house, and those people threw his things out into the street." He continued: "People say that some big gangster was involved or that someone bribed someone. Anyway, no one did anything about it. It was just a small shop. I heard that he got a bit of money by selling off things from it and is now living in some place called the 'Township.' It's a new neighbourhood, not yet fully built." Bashir didn't have the exact address. Then he quoted something Waliullah had once said: "I have lived here fifty years, and it came to nothing."

"I have grown old," Bashir said, starting to become angry. "What can I do? I was barely able to save this place myself. They were after it too. God knows where they get their forged papers. Land is like gold, Bairy, just like gold." He kept on talking, calling me by my childhood name.

"I had advised Waliullah's father to buy some land. It was so cheap back then. But he was always busy with politics. He was a great lover of the People's Party government. And Bhutto, too. He adored them, just like I did. But what did the People's Party do for us?"

I couldn't listen to Bashir any longer, so I left him. Waliullah was gone.

It doesn't mean anything, but sometimes, when I am going to work on a cold winter morning, I imagine Waliullah before me. I place my grey head in his hands and say, "Oh, Waliullah! Breathe. Give me your blessing!"

Bajwa Has Nothing More to Say Now

BAJWA ARRIVES. I've been waiting. He sits for a bit. When the mosquitoes start biting his feet, he says, "Shall we go?"

After days and days of phoning each other, we had finally fixed a meeting at our old coffee house on Lahore's Mall Road. But it wasn't really ours anymore. It had become something entirely new, with a strange face. This was one of our last meetings, when the pleasure of meetings was running low.

The Sufi Fakeer Lal Shah says, "The population has increased, but our meetings have decreased."

There was a time when one wouldn't even think of going home at night, even after midnight.

SOME TIME AGO, while passing along Mall Road, I stopped at the old coffee house, just by chance. That was also a last meeting of sorts. Sometimes the relationships we hold onto become mysterious, and sometimes the mysteries of life themselves become our companions. Most of our journey in this world is in the piercing, naked sunshine. The few companions we find, they are the soft shadows cast by high clouds floating above in the brightness. *How empty the bare light is, how inhospitable.*

The clouds cast their shadow for a moment on a bird floating on the waves of water, and then pass away. Not everything can be remembered, but the smouldering of reminiscence remains. Sometimes it stops you right in your tracks.

I SIT DOWN in the café and don't even bother to order tea. *Where are those evenings at Mall Road now?* Today the black of the night is deeper than soot, and my breath is choked with the fumes of cars. But the mist of remembrance stirs a breath of fresh air amidst the dust.

Uncle Political, as he was called, recognizes me and brings two cups of tea without asking. He figures Bajwa will be here any moment; the second cup is for him.

Of course, if he did come, he wouldn't stay.

"Do not concern yourself with the beloved ... Do not

fall in love," Mitto, the drunkard, always says, gulping a third drink.

This city crawls up my back like a red ant.

IN THE OLD DAYS, Lahore was not so crowded. One could just happen upon an acquaintance on the road. Even people I didn't know seemed familiar in those days. There wasn't any sense of strangeness in the eyes. At the same time, there was no burden of an existing bond. Where did they come from, those emerging relationships, and how were they formed?

"Leave them, throw away all those ties to your heart," the Sufi says. God knows how much Mitto and Chaudhary are going to drink today.

IFFI CHATTA comes to mind—places like this bear the scent of him. Iffi was my best friend in sixth grade. We went to school together. Every day when we were free I took him around on my bike. He was white like *kheer* rice pudding. His father was a police officer in another city and seldom came home; it was rumoured that he kept another woman on the side. Iffi spent most of his time with me, and at night I would drop him home. His house was in the second or third street of our *mohallah*. His mother used to say, "Yes, take him, take him, you are someone to play with. Poor thing." I would ride the bicycle and he would pay a fare: four annas per hour. I had become a big man just like that, though I did make concessions in my fee along the way.

What was school to us? We were not meant to become doctors or engineers. When we passed a class, we moved on to the next. No one pushed us in school, and we didn't make any effort when we got home. When exams were around the corner, we would get a beating from our elders, so we would read a word or two and would pass.

Iffi stuck to me like glue. I couldn't even look after myself, yet he looked to me for shelter. The other boys would pass us by, pinching his cheek hard, and he would cling closer; he was devoted to me. But I became tired of riding the bicycle. I didn't understand what his company meant. When he was the butt of the other boys' jokes, I would sometimes join them. I was his friend, but I wasn't loyal. Then the end came. Faiqi slapped his bottom and gave me a push, saying, "Wa, what a pair!"

I responded with a shallow, evasive laugh.

"You should have slapped his face!" Iffi declared. But he knew that it wasn't possible for me to give the same back to them. After that, he didn't speak with me anymore. He flat out refused. And, after eighth grade, he left school once and for all.

The tragedy of humankind is that when things unveil themselves in the dust, it is too late. I could not forget Iffi, and even in my old age I still remember that street where his house was. Whenever I go to the *mohallah*, I make sure to pass by. I have wandered through it again and again but have never seen him. His street ended at a dead end, and so it still does today. The road is the same, and his house is the same. But where is he?

A WHILE BACK my daughter returned to school after summer vacation and came home crying. She wouldn't tell us what was the matter. She was in seventh grade and was a star student, yet every day she came home in tears and wouldn't discuss it. We couldn't bear to see her weeping. Then suddenly she stopped. And she changed. She appeared a bit older; she had more confidence about her. After some time, my wife told me that our daughter had quarrelled with her best friend. Her friend had become close with another girl and had dropped her. Our daughter implored her friend, but she would not relent. So she gave up, once and for all, and made a new group of friends. After settling in with her new group, she forgot everything. But it all made her a bit harder.

Why does it happen so? People stay in their groups, but then something happens and it falls apart. Why is that?

It's evening on Mall Road. A flock of birds hovers over the High Court. The dark red bricks appear suddenly, like wild pigeons, and melt in a cloud into the grey evening. The smouldering burn of memory descends through a dark, half-open window like a drop of moisture in the late winter air of Phagun. I have experienced this air many times. It has swept through my body time and again, and I have borne it each time.

BAJWA WORE a homespun kurta and traditional open leather sandals. He looked like a poet, but he wasn't and never would be. He was sitting in a corner with Comrade T. T. "Comrade T. T." had been called by various names, first "Comrade Raidva" or Radio, and then "Wireless." Finally, the name "Comrade Table Talker" stuck to him. Later, that was shortened to "T. T." You see, he once contended that the real thing is to be a master "table talker." He used to say that Lenin and Mao Zedong were actually just great table talkers and that all the successful revolutions in the world had been led by such masters. He used to say that, in order to be a good table talker, it was vital that one listen to others carefully, to discover the contradictions in their ideas. Then one should grab those contradictions and play with them. From then on, he became Comrade T. T.

It was Bajwa's first visit to the coffee house; soon the rest of the group would stream in. Comrade T. T. would finish his cigarettes and then it would be time to get some more. Sometimes the whole story got stuck at this point, when someone had to stand up and bring the cigarettes, or when someone had to walk to the counter to ask for tea. At some point, the one who stood up and went felt that he was being looked down upon, and he became irritated. Then he also became the butt of jokes. But Comrade T. T. was never short of people to bring cigarettes for him, and by the time one of his followers started to feel the shallowness of his thesis, the Comrade would have found someone else. He always made friends with people younger than him and educated them. As soon as they became a bit wiser, the first thing they would do is begin to argue with him. His opponents said that he tried to own his friends, didn't meet them on equal footing. He treated them as if they were his pigeons. He took care of them, fostered them, and gave them food. But they didn't return to his roof when he let them fly.

I felt sad for the newcomer. His years seemed to have passed prematurely. He was young but his lips were already darkening from cheap cigarettes. I was at that point planning to leave the group anyway. Comrade T. T. did not want me around. The repetitive, monotonous talks were new only for him. None of it really mattered to him anyway: he had escaped from home and from the narrow behaviours of the parties. He just wanted to be a leading talker. As Bajwa stood up to fetch cigarettes, I offered him one of mine. He hesitated, took one and impulsively sat at my table for a while. Comrade T. T. glared at me with red eyes. It was my last day in that café.

I DIDN'T HAVE TO wait long; Bajwa met me in the old Anarkali Bazaar after just a few days. He lived somewhere near the leather market. Even though his father was a government servant in some department, he looked just like us. I advised to him to be serious and continue his studies, but he kept talking and talking. We went to watch a movie, became friends and remained that way. He wanted to make a "somebody" out of me:

23

I was maybe a step or two ahead in school, and a bit senior to him in the political gatherings. I knew some people before him. But we were both alone and were destined to be friends.

We did everything together, all through those last days of our youth. Friendship, enmities, and politics: these were all the same to us, and we faced them together. People spoke of us in the same breath. We met every day, and night would melt into day again. We were one. One night, after Zia-ul-Haq imposed martial law, someone from the banned Communist Party gave us a thousand pamphlets to throw in every shop on Mall Road. When we finished our rounds, we headed home early in the morning. We weren't frightened at all. During the pro-democracy demonstrations near Anarkali Bazaar on Mall Road, a policeman held me by the collar and started dragging me away. All around us, the lathi charge was going on and there were people and bodies everywhere. It was Bajwa who freed me from the policeman with a jerk and helped me to escape; then he too fled. That police officer chased us up to the old Zamzama Cannon, once used by Maharaja Ranjit Singh and mentioned in Kipling's *Kim*, in the centre of the city. But when he saw the crowd moving against him, he turned back.

Then suddenly Bajwa became angry and stopped talking with me. He just disappeared. Its true, I was a little bitter in those days. But it never occurred to me that he would leave me. I kept hoping and expecting that he would come back. How could he live without me? I am his shadow, his other half. He is not complete without me.

"Friendship is an unscientific relation. It is undialectical," the Master says.

"Friendship is in being there. It is in showing up," says Rang Shah.

THE WINDOW SEEMS to be closing. The night is getting darker. There is no place to sit near Regal Chowk Square. The Mall Luxury, Lord's—all the coffee houses have long since closed. The streets of this city have made me sick; in a corner of the city, somewhere, the shadows of sunken memories continue to flicker like a small flame.

Why had he cut me off? Many things had happened, perhaps, to bring it about. We were equally educated, but I got a job, and he didn't. Perhaps he wasn't angry; maybe he just realized that our time was over, that we had lost the time in which we shared everything we had. Everything had changed: the times, people, and places. And so the city and friends would have to be changed, too. He became silent most of the time and would talk only in close gatherings or with one or two people. Somebody would remind us, "Listen to him, too," but who had the time to listen to others? One had to fight to speak, always cutting somebody else short.

It was as if he had been left behind. He didn't complete his studies on time: when I had become the father of a child, he was still in university. The girl met him there, and she changed his life completely. She married him but took no pride in him. But I shouldn't talk like that: a man can only be happy with a woman. He must concede to her. I thought that he would share his new life with me, but he didn't. So, a gap grew between us. For some time, he did come see me, and his wife somehow opened up a bit too. But it was at just that point that everything was lost. I didn't know what happened, but soon he stopped meeting me once and for all. It looked as if his wife had forbidden him to see me. Once or twice I tried to call his wife on the phone, but she hung up.

When I thought about it, I realized that all this might have been because of Mitto and Murshid, with whom I had begun to drink a lot. After his marriage, whenever he drank, Bajwa would go home chewing paan to hide the scent. I was furious and thought, what kind of a love marriage was it, if a man had to hide such things from his wife?

And then who knows what happened, but the whole city changed. Our friends left, and so many years slipped from our hands, like how a traveller sitting in a night train doesn't know how many cities have been left behind. Seasons changed one after another. But I couldn't forget him. His memory left a subtle pain, a scar on my heart. I was a lonely soul with only empty days before me. Why did he leave me? Sometimes while passing through the city I would imagine him: he is right over there, riding a motorcycle, but unrecognizable because of his helmet. He used to go to political gatherings, so I thought we might meet at one and chat.

But he couldn't be found. Someone told me that he had washed his hands of everything. His hair was gone now, and he looked old.

NOT TOO LONG BACK, when the lawyers' movement was emerging, I too joined the demonstrations with a couple of friends. Old habits die hard. We gathered on Mall Road and shouted slogans condemning those in power at the Lahore High Court and Charing Cross, and then dispersed. Our old lawyer friends had called us to join them: they thought that the dice had finally been cast in our favour. One day we joined the procession in the hottest hour of the day. The female lawyers were wearing black glasses and holding umbrellas; everyone carried bottles of mineral water. But the vigour of the slogans was no less strong.

After crossing Regal Chowk Square, we surged forward, and saw a crowd of people and journalists at the overhead bridge of the Panorama Shopping Centre. They were waiting there with flowers in their hands, and when the procession passed under the bridge, they scattered a rain of flowers over it. From the end of procession, I could see the people throwing flowers from above. All at once, I saw Bajwa among them. *Was it him, or someone else?* It looked just like him from a distance. He was holding a huge basket of flowers and was slowly throwing them over the people passing under the bridge. He appeared thin and weak. I waved my hands, recognizing him from far away; he threw flowers over us when

27

we passed. The flowers clung to my hair and the petals slipped in my pocket. I didn't brush them off. I dreamt of Bajwa's flowers for many days after that: I am passing under a bridge and Bajwa is throwing flowers from above.

A life has passed but the fragrance of Bajwa's flowers still hangs in the air.

Dead Man's Float

AND SO IT HAPPENED that the house remained within his consciousness, haunting his dreams.

If he dreamt of the dead then there they were, in that house; if he dreamt of the living, they were in the same house again. It all happened in front of that house, in the streets of the neighbourhood or nearby. He had moved from here to there, lived in various places, and had even gone abroad—but even there he dreamt of that same house and those very streets. The twenty-one years he had spent in the house had devoured all the years of his life since. And that was the real tragedy that haunted him: it was not his own house and so he was forced to leave it.

He didn't return for many years after he left. The new tenants continued to call him to visit, until they themselves didn't live there anymore. Even the newcomers who followed them also left. Then one more tenant came, and he too didn't stay. Finally, someone bought the old house, demolished it, and built it anew. The new owner built a grand house with a novel design, more than three times as large as the old one, with multiple stories and a towering gate in front. When he saw the new house, the pain that was ever slumbering in his deepest unconscious was awakened. He let out a long cold sigh.

The first house was utterly different. It had three rooms on the ground floor, with a kitchen on the side, and a tiny courtyard. Underneath the stairs going to the second floor, there was a room for bathing. The toilet was at the top of house; that's how it was done in the 1960s, when it was built. There was a big room on right side on the second storey, and on the left, a kitchen and a small room.

He stood looking at the new house. He had the old one in his heart: he was watching the new one through the old one. When he could only see the old one and not the new, he became even more dejected. Living in the city so many years, he had finally come to revisit his old house in the old neighbourhood.

It is our tragedy that we are not allowed to live in the places where we are born and become ourselves, the dreams of which remain alive within us. The beginning of our sojourn on this earth is like a blue sky. Time turns it grey. But remembrance turns that ash colour into a deep smoky blue. This is the place between dreams and reality, where we keep living and dying.

Just a little time has passed, and the rain has stopped. But there is still a touch of water in the hard, piercing air that thrashes his face, making it cold and wet. The wind continues to blow.

All the world has changed and keeps on changing. The wide streets have become narrow and the narrow ones extremely thin: all the old houses are being demolished and new ones are being built. The streets have been raised higher and the older houses have become new, and the new ones even newer: modest houses have just disappeared. The houses one could go to and from without any hesitation now seem so strange, so distant, so far out of reach. The soggy air blows fast in the silent street, making an eerie noise. Then a bike or car manages to wade through, splashing water, or it turns back: where have all the old vendors of the *mohallah* gone now?

At the first turn of the lane, a slightly larger road beyond is transforming into a major bazaar. First came the burger kiosk, then a small motorcycle mechanic shop, and then the car repair garage. Next came the grocery store and then a stationery shop full of notebooks and pencils. After the kiosk for paan, chewing tobacco, and cigarettes was opened, you would always see the boys standing outside it. But that all happened many years after he and his family were forced to leave. For so many years even after that, there was just a shop or two nearby. From there one could get anything, from a small needle to cigarettes.

A very old car, the cheapest one could imagine, wanders haltingly, as if it is about to stop. But then it comes very slowly, passing near him. A young man and his wife sit in the front seat: in the back, two children and a woman. She catches his eye somehow. He looks closely at her: she is elderly, or no, perhaps middle-aged. Their eyes meet for a moment. At first both are surprised, then upset. Then both heave a deep sigh in which there is a kind of a moan. They both pretend not to have seen what they have seen. And perhaps they didn't.

If she could stop for a while and could have an exchange of greetings, would somebody shoot her? She may still think herself too good for that, but even I have a better car than her now. In the old days she held her nose up high. She's gotten old over the last few years, keeping an eye on her adolescent daughters. But now they too have gotten old, all without getting married. We were nothing in those days; leaving one or two families aside, all the boys were underprivileged.

He had internalized and lived her face so many nights and days, cherished dreams of each and every curve of her body. But she never once spoke with him.

Mornings became evenings in front of her home. How proud she was of her beauty and status; how rich she appeared at that time. After all her father was a minor servant in some government department and they did have a motorcycle; in the whole *mohallah* they had the only one. They were more prosperous than others, but what are they now? He has more than them, but he knows that no matter how prosperous he might become, he would never have her. Before, he couldn't have her because he was beneath her. Now, what was it? Time. It is like a rebellious pigeon who flies away but never comes back to sit at your roof.

What did we get by thinking about "lower" and "higher"? Separation and loneliness, nothing more.

The evening descended, and for a long time he wanders in his old *mohallah*. He doesn't come across a single person from his old days. The rain has worn off the old fading whitewash from the walls, and the ancient dirt-coloured bricks are emerging from underneath, as if time itself has unearthed them.

A little movement appears in the silent streets: suddenly it speeds up, and then it slows down again. It is as if the rain has slowed everyone down, empty and helpless: the sharp wind has driven everyone from the streets. A blanket of darkness secretly tries to steal everything close to him, and a dim light leaks out from the doors and windows of the nearby houses. Two young men are walking along briskly, talking in loud, boisterous voices. They slow down for a moment when they see him, but when they don't recognize him, they move on, absorbed in their fun. Who knows how long he has been wandering there; now the darkness has fully descended, enveloping the world. "Go home now," something within him says. "Home." He looks at the old house, where now a new one is standing. "Nobody recognizes you. Look. It is late. If someone stopped and spoke with you, then maybe you would wake out of your reverie."

The night has settled into the streets, and the wind of fear passes through his heart. He is soaking wet. What if somebody were to ask where he is going, which house he is looking for, whom he intends to see? Cold, wet fear sends waves through his inner core. He trembles. Fear: that fear of being unrecognized in the night, in the cold, wet wind. It brings to mind that night he passed sleeping in a park while he was abroad, on his own. That night, fully unpassed. The whole of it stands before him.

That night twenty-nine years ago when, after fleeing from the hunger of his home with some friends, lost in the greed of earning in Europe, he had gone to Rome and got stuck. After months of sleeping in the streets and the underground Metro stations, he was supposed to sleep that night in a real bed. Masood had given him the key. Masood too was from Lahore, and from the same *mohallah*, Krishan Nagar. He had been living in Rome for many years and had become like a local. But whenever Masood got drunk, he used to repeat two things again and again. First: "I didn't mean to live in Rome; I always thought I would go to England or America. I am just stuck in Rome for nothing." He had been living there for many years. It was said that his aunt lived in England, but who knows why she did not bring him there. Second, he used to recall his mother. She was probably living alone in Lahore in some rented room in a corner of Krishan Nagar; he sent her some US dollars every year or so. I never asked about his father, and he never spoke of him. After drinking, he would speak only of his mother: "My mother must be alone, all alone. She wanted me to get married. She must be waiting for me." Masood was around thirty-three or thirty-five years old then, and I had not yet reached twenty.

Masood met me at Piazza Navona. We had arrived in Rome in summer, but now the cold was piercing. We were three friends without a clue, like fools, with just a few dollars in our pockets. We made our way on the road from Afghanistan to Iran, then to Turkey; then from Istanbul we took the Oriental Express through Yugoslavia and arrived in Rome on a five-day visa. Shooky went to work on a ship, but I was refused because I wore glasses. Manzali got a job in another city and was thrilled because a Filipina was working there with him.

Piazza Navona is a famous tourist place in Rome. It has a large open area with beautiful statues in a circle; beautiful old buildings surround them. There is a wide courtyard of old grey brick, and grey pigeons are always hovering, picking their food off the ground. All around there are cafés, restaurants, and bars, where tourists sit all day long soaking in the sun. I came upon the place by chance, wandering all day in the city, and then started coming every day.

The hippie movement was at its peak, and it was here that I bumped into Jhangi from Karachi. He opened a kiosk there every evening. But the kiosk was illegal and sometimes when it was raided by the authorities, I would recall the raids of the Lahore Municipal Corporation back home. Jhangi had been living in Rome with his family for many years. His wife would make handmade toys all day and he used to sell them at Piazza Navona in his kiosk. The toys were made of colourful pieces of cloth and were very attractive. There was a sign written on a hard sheet lying near by them: "Hand Made."

When he would set up his kiosk, I would stand near him, with nothing to do. I wandered all day alone, without any place to sleep, with nothing to do. We got free food from church, and we could sleep in the empty, broken houses of the hippies. Most of the hippies used to live in condemned buildings. They would break into abandoned houses, seize them, and squat there.

Seeing me jobless, Jhangi suggested that I work with him. I accepted at once. He gave his own kiosk to me and started to set up another one. But I still couldn't find any place to live. To live anywhere you needed a passport or some other papers that the police called "*documenti.*" My passport was already with the police, and they were keeping an eye on me until the day they could find enough money on me for an air ticket so they could deport me. At that point, I did have some money because of the work, but there was still no place to live.

Jhangi would say to me every day, "I would take you home, but my wife wouldn't like it."

Then one day Jhangi introduced me to Masood, who was also from Lahore. Then we discovered that we were from the same *mohallah*. Masood lived at a very cheap place, but he still was not able to afford it. So now he was hopeful that we could share the rent. Next day we met in the sunshine, and he showed me the place. It was something like an old store, covered in disintegrating plaster and whitewash. There was an old bed on one side and on the other an iron bed frame. That was supposed to be my bed: he laid some worn out foam on it, spread out some kind of old sheet, and then gave me an old blanket. You could call it my first home abroad. I lived there many months. But I lost my way getting there on the first night.

Counting out the money with Jhangi at Piazza Navona, it was normal to stay until midnight or beyond. I had to return the kiosk to him. It was made of steel and had to be separated, each and every part, so that it was easy to put in the trunk of his car. After counting out the money and finishing the work and having one or two shots of whisky from the bar near the station—which remained open all night—it never occurred to me that I might not actually know the way to the place where I was supposed to sleep. I went to the place I thought I was going, but I couldn't find the place that Masood had shown me in the morning. There was supposed to be a big, open gate-like door somewhere, and then after passing through it, a tiny, narrow verandah.

Turning left and walking down some stairs, there was supposed to be the store-like room. If I could just find that door-like gate, I could find my way.

My breath caught in my throat. It was the middle of the night. Police cars passed by me slowly. After wandering and wandering, I reached a place where I was sure that I would find Masood: a corner on the main road that would lead to the street with the big gate. He would pass by, late, and we'd walk together to the house. I tucked into a shadow.

Time passed and Masood didn't appear, and I realized I had not only lost the street but the neighbourhood. Cars stopped making their usual noises and drunken couples came out, standing together, hugging and kissing each other. I was becoming more and more afraid. What if one of them phoned the police to say that some South Asian man was standing in the street at midnight, appearing suspicious . . . ? So I kept walking on in silence. It was only through walking and walking that I could save myself from the police.

Walking like that, on and on, I don't know where I finally ended up. At last I came to a big road with traffic passing in both directions. There was light all around—or perhaps night was just coming to an end—and there appeared to be a park in the distance. It was a time in Europe, or at least in Rome, when you could spend a night in a park and police wouldn't bother you. Though I was dead tired because of walking so long, the hope of a park sharpened the pace of my feet. But it was not a park: it was just an empty area, a kind of square. But at that point I couldn't even stand anymore, so I sat down there on the grass: when a man is hungry there is even pleasure in drinking water. At last I leaned against a lamp and slept right there. That was, in truth, my first home abroad.

WALKING IN THE OLD *mohallah*, it is as if he is standing in front of her house. At that time it appeared to be such a big house. But it was just a small house on a tiny lot. It was old, from the time before Partition, and no one had spent anything on it for many years. Mud oozed from the fissures in the walls.

The dark night thickened.

The wet air created an unseen, untouched wire in the extreme darkness of the night. The blue flame of remembrance has scorched every thing inside. In old times, when out late, he would stop beneath her window and his friends would go on ahead; it seemed to him that someone was awakening behind the window.

Our beginning is like a blue sky; time makes it dull and grey. Remembrance turns it into the deep blue of evening, before it becomes a thick night. There is some other place between dream and reality where we live and die.

It appears that her window has opened for the first and last time. A long straight line of light stretches down the road, making the drenched road shine like glass. From behind the window where the light leaks out, a voice seems to emerge.

"Go home, Bairy, and sleep."

Pigeons, Ledges, and Streets

YOU COULD SAY that this story is about Gamay, the
pigeons, the rooftop ledges, or me. But really it is the
story of Maasi Ayshan. Not too long ago, I tried to visit
my ancestral home in Batala, back in India, and, searching everywhere for the family home, I finally happened
upon the home of Maasi Ayshan. At least I think I did.
Whenever Mother used to talk about our Batala home,
Maasi's house would always come up. "Our house was
on a small hill, and my brother's courtyard was on the
left side of the bazaar. On the right was Maasi's." Our
homes were always mentioned in the same breath.

The two men who were sent by the doctor-poet of Batala to help me find the house were exasperated. "Sir-ji, sometimes you say right, sometimes left."

"We'll find it. There is lots of time. Why are you in such a rush?"

They were running me ragged and would not let me stand in any one place for a minute. All I wanted to do was stroll through the streets and neighbourhoods. Whether or not I find the house, who cares? This was the place we left behind.

"Your home was on the right, or the left?"

"It was here, somewhere in these streets."

Maasi Ayshan's house was on the street in front of our house. Reaching out across time, the voice of my mother flows through me from within.

Maasi Ayshan's house in Lahore was near the last bus stop in Krishan Nagar, our old *mohallah*, just a few streets from our house. It was a bit far off if you went straight from the market on the main road, but if you went through the lanes, it was quite close. After Partition, their family arrived after being robbed and abused all along the way. They hung onto any place they could get. But then Maasi made a mistake. She settled into her house on the second floor and let others take the ground floor. It was an old house, decaying before our eyes until it dwindled down to almost nothing. But for Maasi it was all she had, so she wouldn't leave it. Some time passed in the warmth of sharing with the residents of the lower floor, but at last they brought a case in court. Maasi was enraged.

"I was the one who let them in. 'Okay, you can stay on the lower floor, and we can stay upstairs.' Who kept a careful eye at that time? Any house could be repossessed. We all thought that we'd be going back, anyway. Who thought they were going to sit here forever? So many houses were empty. God bless your uncle, who worked in Lord Sahib's office in the Secretariat. He showed us so many places. My husband, Popa's father, said, 'Now that we have settled here, this is fine.' Could we ever have thought something like this was going to happen to us?"

Uncle, Maasi Ayshan's husband, had already passed away before we knew what was what. Perhaps that was at the root of my mother's and Maasi's secret, shared pain: that both of their husbands had passed away in the prime of their youth. Maasi had three sons. Two went abroad and one had stayed with her. Nothing was known about the eldest. All we knew was that he was in some snow-filled country somewhere. But he had neither sent a letter, nor made an appearance in all those years. We didn't know when or where he had gone. The second one was in England. He would always send spending money back home, and it was that which kept the house running. Maasi's first son was born in Batala, which went to India at Partition, but the others were born in Lahore. The youngest was in university and was four or five years older than me. When the military dictator got his comeuppance, he was at the head of the procession against him in our *mohallah*. But we school children were not allowed to go beyond the Laat Sahib's office, the Punjab Secretariat, and he would send us away with threats.

When the new People's Party's government came into power, Maasi's son became enmeshed in it. He used to come home late at night. We had been going to Maasi's house since our childhood, so we could all share in our Batala past. After her husband passed away and her two sons went abroad, Maasi's house—which was already quite old—was empty too. The youngest son would go to university and Maasi was left alone all day at home. We used to bring groceries and look after her. After every second or third day, some cooked food would be sent to her, or she herself would come home and gossip with my mother for hours. When we would go to her house, she would be waiting for us. On the second floor, there were two big rooms, a tiny courtyard and to one side, a small room. Gamay and Rakhi lived in that small room.

Oh yes, I was going to tell the tale of Gamay and the pigeons, wasn't I?

The tale of Gamay, like our ancestral home in Batala, is fading away. But she was there throughout our childhood. She used to wash the family dishes in Krishan Nagar. But Gamay's story couldn't be completed without Rakhi. Just as in Batala while searching for my own home, I was also looking for the home of Maasi Ayshan, so with the story of Gamay, I have to tell the tale of Rakhi too.

Passing through the streets of Krishan Nagar, I could never forget Gamay and Rakhi. Rakhi would hold onto the edge of Gamay's *kameez* from behind, and Gamay would put her face straight forward and rush on; Rakhi would follow behind her on bare feet with almost running steps, clutching her small cloth bundle, as if she were also a part of Gamay's body. I can't draw a picture of just one of them in my mind. They were one body, two souls. Neither had any relatives or connections. They would live with whomever would have them. Then, after much quarrelling wherever they went, they came to Maasi Ayshan's. There at last they became part of her family. As long as Maasi lived, they lived with her in that house.

After many years when Auntie Appa Ulfat came from America, I asked her about Gamay. She was very surprised, "Don't you remember? We met her at the same time." But then she told as much as she knew.

"I saw Gamay when she first came from the village. She was well off, as far as her family background was concerned. By caste she was a *malik*, a landowner, and they had lands near the Ravi River. When she was married, she kept Rakhi with her. Rakhi was one of God's special people—you know, something was not quite right with her—perhaps since birth. Or maybe she got that way later. Who knows? But nobody did anything for her, until Gamay. After Gamay got married, her husband threw her out because of Rakhi. "You can keep Rakhi, or live with me," he said. After she quarrelled with her brothers, too, she came with Rakhi to live at Maasi Ayshan's. It is said that there was also a dispute with the brothers over land. But she never discussed it. We always saw her at Maasi Ayshan's home. Nobody ever came to see her."

Fair-skinned, Gamay was a sturdy peasant woman, with a full, strong body and a ring in her nose. No one dared even look at her the wrong way. She, in contrast, would never look at anyone. She was always quietly lost in her work. There was something on her face, something in between anger and nervousness; you couldn't quite call it annoyance. It seemed as if there was something unacceptable around her, or a sense of the world's indifference. There was also a kind of sadness. As the Sufi poet Madho Lal Hussain said, "Neither happiness nor grief should find their place in the heart."

Gamay used to do only one thing: wash dishes. She wouldn't touch anything else. Scrubbing or wiping or something like that she would never do. Sometimes women would get fed up, but she didn't let anything bother her. She would say, "If you want your dishes washed, great. Otherwise, it is up to you." She would do her work with great attention, however. For her, there was only her work.

Rakhi was truly touched by God. Physically, she was like a skeleton, without a bit of flesh on her body. She would just keep waving her hands in front of her face madly as if she was talking to or calling someone, or trying to stop them. I don't know which, but it was either

fearsome or fearful. Or she would just laugh, showing her teeth. She wouldn't leave Gamay for a single
moment. When Gamay would wash dishes, she would
sit close to her and open the small sack she carried and
laugh, showing her teeth. She had hidden all the world's
treasures in that bag. There were hair clips, hair pins,
a soap box, empty packets of cigarettes, a toothbrush,
pillow covers, small children's toys, glass beads, empty
tiny bottles of scent, small empty nail polish bottles,
empty powder boxes, and God knows what else.

She wouldn't allow anyone to touch her bag. Whenever anything got lost, everybody would say, "Search
Rakhi's bag, it must be there!" But you would have to
get a hand on it first! If you tried to take the bag, Rakhi
would try to hide behind Gamay, clinging to her. Gamay
would pay her no mind and remain absorbed in her
work. In the end, if you tried to snatch the bag forcibly, she would desperately throw it away. All the things
inside would scatter. Then you and whoever else was
behind the mischief would feel ashamed. You'd be forced
to collect all the things yourself and try to give her back
the bag. But then Rakhi would stand apart and wouldn't
touch it. By the next day, though, she would have the bag
back in her armpit, carrying it everywhere.

There was a small room or storage closet on top of
Maasi's house. The pigeons lived there. No one knows
from where and when the pigeons had settled there.
Maybe they were from before Partition. But we used to
call that room "the pigeon house." For us, it was a place

of freedom, but for Maasi, it was her rooftop. Maasi
would stay in her room downstairs all day and we would
spend all day on the roof. We would let the pigeons fly,
make wagers on which would fly best, and play games.
There were so many pigeons you couldn't count them.
The cooing of pigeons and the slight sting of the smell
of their droppings permeated the area in all directions.
It would come to you, stinging your nose, as you climbed
the stairs to Maasi's house. The more respectable members of our family stopped going to Maasi's: why would
one go there, just to smell pigeon droppings? If a woman
visited, she would pull her *dupatta*, her long scarf, over
her nose while talking. In truth, that was all just a pre-
tence. They did not want to go to see Maasi anyway. She
was not of their class.

Every three or six months, Maasi would bribe us, and
we would put on our shorts or hitch up our lungis to
wash the rooftop while the pigeons soared above. We
would fill and carry up buckets of water from below and
soon all the stairs down to the bottom would be flowing with water and pigeon droppings. Whoever would
come would lift the legs of his shalwar and back away
saying, "Oh my God, forgive me." The people from the
ground floor would have something to say about it too.
The pigeons would fly high and then they would come
down again all at once on the roof or would fly low
above it like a cloud. Whenever the pigeons would take
off like this, everybody would be surprised: "How can
Maasi keep so many pigeons?" The huge flying mass of

Maasi's pigeons hung in the sky and dimmed the sun, creating a huge shadow. Any bit of bread that was left in our house was earmarked for Maasi's pigeons. Quite a few houses around would send old, dry bread for them. It is Maasi's pigeons that remain in our minds now, flying and cooing.

Sometimes a cat would come and launch an attack. If by chance the door of the pigeon house was left open, or someone had forgotten to fix the latch, the cat would come upon the birds in the middle of the night. The story of the cat's attack would make its way around the neighbourhood for days. The children of our *mohallah* would come to see the dead and wounded pigeons over and over again. Maasi would burst into tears, and we could not hold back our cries. When the cat attacked at night, it was as if we could hear the voices of thousands of feathers sobbing heavily, as if some huge wounded bird was circling the house. It was terrifying. Then, after completing her task, the cat would disappear into the shadows. Behind her, she would leave broken pigeon feathers, the dark red splatter of blood on the walls, half-dead naked pigeon bodies, and the writhing and wriggling of infant birds and broken eggs. Then we would bring buckets full of water to wash the walls. The pigeon house couldn't be locked so that the pigeons would continue to come in and out to peck at their food as we worked.

I was free in those days. After taking the basic high school exams at the end of tenth grade, which decide who can study further and who cannot, I roamed here and there. Everything looked new and full, and my heart longed to act, to *do something*, with love and care and passion. Emotions rose like the pigeons to touch the skies; my eyes filled with the deep blue colour, spilling over. One needs proof of one's existence at that age, more than ever before or again. This is that age when the lover weeps in hiding if their beloved turns away. When the newly grown hair on the face starts to look good but is accompanied by the desire to shave it away. Life never again changes as much as it does in tenth grade.

Popa's room was filled with books. He was never at home; God knows when he used to read them. I read Gorky's *Mother* from among his books. Those books brought me awareness of the idea of sharing wealth for the sake of all and understanding of the pain of the dispossessed. Popa was frail; he was quiet and furtive. He thought of me as a child. Deprived of blood, his face burned like smoke; he was fond of tea and smoking. He didn't take interest in any household activity. Every once in a while, his friends would come on a Sunday, smoke too many cigarettes, drink a lot of tea, and gossip. The dustbin would fill with cigarette butts and the teacups would fill with ash. His mother had nothing but love for her son's friends. Let it be—at least he is at home this way.

Maasi wanted to find some way to get her son married. The first two sons had flown away like pigeons who wouldn't return. Maasi would sound out the older women of the *mohallah* about each of the eligible girls and would then sit with my mother for long hours, reviewing each young girl's background and potential. She would inquire particularly after those girls in Lahore who had come from Batala and Gurdaspur, now in India. Then a strange thing happened. Someone—either one of Maasi's close relatives or from farther afield—sent a young girl to live with Maasi. Her name was Naina. Her mother sent her, saying that Maasi couldn't do her household work anymore.

If she had come earlier to live with Maasi, I wouldn't have noticed. But I was at that age when I would sit on the rooftop all day long and peer into other houses, just for the chance to see something. The girl was nice enough looking, medium height, with a colour neither pale nor dark, but somewhere in between. She was like a wild pigeon. She came to serve Maasi, but as time passed, Maasi decided that she wanted her son to marry her. But Popa had no time for it; he didn't even look at her. I had developed a great connection with Popa in those days. We were like brothers. Now sometimes I think it was all because he was one of those men who is anti-women. He used to say that a man would lose his resolve if he became too close to a woman. Or maybe not. Maybe he had set his heart on someone at the university. Naina would come in when we were sitting and talking in some room and he would wink at me. Then everything would get lost in laughter and noise. She was otherwise very hardworking and, whenever I used to come to see Maasi, she would always have some job or other for me to do. Do this, do that; bring this from the bazaar, or bring that. She was the same age as Popa, just a bit older than me by three or four years.

An unusual scent wafted from her hair and a light burned in her eyes. It looked to me as if she might have been weeping, because it seemed that her eyes were always wet. She seemed as if she was very fragile, dying of hunger. I didn't understand what was beautiful in her. Yet she looked so good and sweet, and my heart longed for her to remain near me. If only she could live forever at Maasi's house. Perhaps her presence alone was her beauty. Her cheeks were sunken in, and there wasn't a hint of flesh on her body. But Popa was just like that too.

The issue of Gamay's marriage came up again at that time. Some men and women came to look her over. The thing I didn't like was that no matter how much I brought for them to eat, they ate it all. I disliked them, such ill-mannered people. Then, all of a sudden, the marriage date was fixed. I was very surprised that Gamay would leave forever. Nobody thought of Rakhi. Everybody had forgotten her, as if standing before all of us, she had faded away and disappeared. Then Gamay said: "She will live with me, will always be with me. Why should I leave her? I don't trust anybody to take care of her."

Gamay dug out an old trunk and from inside appeared jewellery and other clothes. God knows where it came from. Our family also lent its support. After polishing the trunk, everything was neatly arranged in it. After sewing some suits, the ritual of the dowry was also completed. Gamay's husband-to-be was a widower and there had been some negotiating over the fostering of two or three children from his previous wife. They all came in a horse-drawn cart, the Maulvi Sahib, the cleric, recited some Qur'anic verses, and just like that, Gamay was seen off by all. There was no trumpet or clarinet playing. All of it was done quietly. Maasi's home then became desolate and quiet, and Naina took charge of the house.

One day I came to Maasi's and heard loud talking from outside. It seemed that some guest had arrived. A handsome young boy wearing a tight-fitting sweater was talking animatedly and Naina, Maasi, and Popa were laughing loudly in the front room. I learned that he had come from Karachi for a tour of Lahore. He was also from among Maasi's relatives, like Naina, and was training with the Air Force. I was astonished to see Naina so enamoured of him. She served him with relish. I was in no place to say anything, but I didn't like it one bit. I didn't go to Maasi's place for many days after that. I just wandered around, grief-stricken. I didn't even visit the pigeons. Maasi kept calling for me, sending messages through my mother.

At last I went one day. I found out that Naina had gone to watch a movie with the guest from Karachi. When would this bastard leave? He had just got stuck, like glue. I was there when they came back, laughing and dilly-dallying along the way after watching the movie. Naina disappeared after seeing me and didn't face me. Maasi told me that their guest would leave the next day.

The next morning I got the message from Maasi that a cat had attacked the pigeons during the night. I took a long time in coming. I had never done that before. The guest was ready to go. He was wearing his tight sweater, too much cologne, and was at full alert, guarding his suitcase, waiting for the taxi. He got a quick hug from Maasi, shook hands with me like a stranger, stepped downstairs and went away in the car standing near the door. It was rare to hire a taxi for personal use at that time. Then he was gone, happy and carefree. I swear to God, what did we have to do with him anyway?

I climbed quickly to the rooftop. The walls of the pigeon house were covered with blood. Half-dead, wounded bodies and broken feathers were scattered all around. I couldn't see Naina anywhere. I became absorbed in washing and cleaning. I brought buckets of water from below and started to wash the pigeon house and walls. Then I heard sighs from behind the pigeon house. Naina was squatting on the floor, her heels touching the ground, her face tucked into her legs. She was sighing and sobbing, hesitantly and silently. Her thin body trembled. I was shocked and confused. I kept doing the only thing I could do: bring the buckets of water and wash the blood. I washed the blood spots with the water, gathered all the broken feathers, swept them into a pile and chased away all the pigeons. I shooed them from the ledges on the rooftop, waving a stick like a mad man. In a moment, all of them seemed to be touching the sky, high above. If anyone of them tried to come down, I became mad again, running to chase them off. "Go! Fly away, fly away, fly . . . away."

Tired, I stood up near the ledge. After a long time, Naina came and stood near me. She put her hand on the ledge, watching the flying pigeons rise into the sky. Her face lowered, cheeks hollow and sucked in, like a dead pigeon's body. The evening slowly descended from Krishan Nagar's old ashen ledges to chase away the dim light of the streets and was lost. Dark ledges and dark alleys lay below. Naina, the ledges, and the evening were all at once blended into a single colour.

The local street person, Father Time as he was called, walked by in the street below, lifting one arm high on one side and knocking it against the doors of the houses in the lane. He threw and beat his other arm forcefully in every direction, swinging and waving it. He yelled in a high strong voice, "Go to you mother and ask her, what time is it? Go to your sister, and ask her, what time is it?"

We would tease Father Time, "Father, what time is it?" and then he'd start naming the asker's mother and sister.

I don't know what I was thinking. I slowly placed my hand on hers. She started and turned back. Her eyes burned like the descending sun at dusk. "You . . ."

"You . . . you wash the pigeon shit! If the cat attacks, you wash away the blood—the dead bodies . . ."

She cried out, trembling with anger, and raised her hands, gesticulating. Then she made a loud sound with her feet and pounded down the stairs from the roof.

Suddenly, there was a commotion below in the street: "She's come, she's come! . . . Our Gamay has returned!" The cart stopped at Maasi's door. The coachman lifted the polished trunk and put it at our door. Gamay and Rakhi descended from the back side of the cart, the same as they always were, and exactly identical, joined together like an old painting on a wall, hanging in time. They arrived at the door. Gamay and Rakhi had returned from their newly married home, never to go back again. It was the same old story: "If you want to live here, Rakhi must go." But how could Gamay abandon Rakhi?

The next day when I came to Maasi's in the afternoon, Naina had already left.

The household work would again be taken care of by Gamay. As long as Maasi lived, Gamay lived with her.

We would tease Rakhi about marriage from time to time: "Let's arrange Rakhi's wedding! Let's marry her off!" What an idea. "Ah ji! The bridegroom will come in the marriage procession for Rakhi! Ah ji! The young bridegroom will be here soon!" And she would want to die of embarrassment, and hide herself in her sack, away from everybody. Gamay never again raised the issue of marriage for herself, nor did anybody mention it again. She passed through the remainder of her youth at Maasi's house, washing dishes.

Finally, when his hero Zulfikar Bhutto was hanged, Popa got caught. At first, we were too afraid to go to the police station. We couldn't get any information about where he was being kept. Finally, Maasi and I exhausted ourselves looking in the courts and police stations. Maasi couldn't be stopped. She went out to take part in Bhutto's funeral when the whole street was full of policemen. The rest of the women from the *mohallah* climbed the stairs to the rooftop, which was covered in pigeon droppings, to watch the funeral procession. After a year, when Popa was freed from prison, Maasi reluctantly sent him to England to stay with her other son, so that when the country finally became free again, he could come back. How much time would it take for the country to get freedom? We'd been through all this before.

The sorrow of her son's departure was still fresh when Maasi lost the twenty-five-year-long court case over the ownership of the house initiated by those living on the ground floor. But then she appealed, so it took many years for them to take possession. By that time, the house was about to collapse. There were one or two men living in the lower portion who were waiting to move in. They kept saying: Accept one or two lakhs and let it be over. But Maasi didn't listen. The floors in the rooms were cracked and the roof was decaying. Only the stairs were intact, but only up to the second storey. There were columns and wooden bars to support the stairs leading to the top of the roof. Gamay's small rooms on top were hardly standing, supported only by wooden planks, and there were holes in the floor. Our own family house was also sold by our uncles to build a bungalow in Defence, an elite area in Lahore. But Maasi's Krishan Nagar house was still there. I used to go to court to see the trial; the case might have lingered on even longer but eventually Maasi herself breathed her last, and with her the case died.

Gamay lived with Maasi till the end. Three women alone, in that ruined house.

Maybe this story is really about Gamay, who remained committed to Rakhi to the last. She is still alive, and lives near the old graveyard in Krishan Nagar with Rakhi. Gamay always could find some kind of Maasi Ayshan to clean for.

My mother's voice doesn't leave me: "Maasi Ayshan's house was there, opposite our house, at the other side of the street." Searching for my own house in Batala, I think I was really searching for Maasi Ayshan's house.

When I returned from my trip to India to see our ancestral home, the only survivor among my six uncles came to see pictures. Seeing one of them, and relishing the pleasure of recognizing it, he said at once, "This street used to go straight to Maasi Ayshan's house."

The Beak of the
Green Parrot,
Submerged
in the River

WE HAD BEEN sent to a remote schoolhouse on official duty. I arrived with my staff just before evening. We asked the watchman to open the rooms and began to assess each one to see which might fit our needs.

One room was already occupied by soldiers who had arrived before us. They were stationed here on duty, like us. The next day, this was to be a polling station and votes would be cast.

The school was a bit removed from the village. Its newly constructed building was hidden in deep green shadow among the dense trees, with carefully arranged flower beds and sharply cut flat grass in front. Its walls, doors, and windows were painted with a new layer of crimson paint. A strange mist emerged out of the deep shadows, covering the whole place, as if somebody had placed crimson toffee on deep green paper, and it had begun to melt.

That night the school's watchman told us that the white men of the World Bank had come here once. The place seemed so beautiful to them that they recently arranged for the reconstruction of the school. The old school building was there, alongside the new one, but it had become dilapidated. The doors and windows had disappeared, and there were so many holes in the roof that it too was almost gone. The new school had three big rooms and one small room for a headmaster. The watchman didn't have the key for the headmaster's room. Of the three remaining rooms, one was already occupied by the soldiers. So we had to make do with the remaining two. We had to be on duty at seven the next morning, after spending the night there.

I met him in front of the military men's room. His other colleagues were out and about, while he stood at full alert at the door in his uniform. I shook hands with him with a laugh and peeped inside the room. "Have a look," he said. I was interested in his company. Why not? We were there together through tomorrow; anyway, shared work creates a kind of relationship among people. Maybe things seemed like that to him, too, because he returned the warmth of my greeting.

There were four beds in the room. The bed sheets were neatly arranged over them, and new blankets had been folded and left on the ends. The careful habits of soldiers, driven deep into their very being.

There was a profound cold in that place, born of the deepening winter months of Poh and early Magh, the thick trees, and the lack of people. The cold passed directly through from one's feet. We sat on the beds in front of each other. I took out a packet of cigarettes and offered him one. He took the cigarette, looked down, and smiled like a child. Then he suddenly gazed at the door and a shadow of fear crossed his face. He began to light the cigarette, but then looked at me and a wave of shame seemed to pass through him. He stood up all at once and said: "I'm on duty, I'll smoke it later. I am on guard now. We can't leave the arms unguarded." I stood up with him.

And so it was that I met the first of the four military men who had come on duty with us.

My offer of a cigarette, and his not smoking it but keeping it for later, created a secret bond between us that continued till the end. Later he told me that while on duty, soldiers are not allowed to accept the offer of cigarettes from non-military men or from strangers.

The other three military men returned soon. One of them was the Havaldar, a non-commissioned junior officer, and he was in charge. The Havaldar too was a good man. When he needed to, he acted the proper officer, but he was also fond of gossip. In addition to the four soldiers, there were four of us; more were supposed to arrive early in the morning. We arranged chairs and tables according to our requirements and sent a message to the village headman, or Lambardar, to arrange for food and provisions for our stay that night. We arranged our papers and other work until late. Our job was to begin early in the morning, and we all were tense. During elections and the casting of ballots, who knows how many envelopes would have to be filled. After the voting finished, there would be no time to do anything, so all the paperwork had to be prepared in advance.

When I finished my work after midnight and was finally going to sleep, I heard a sweet voice singing from soldier's room:

The water of Ghallapur bungalow, plunging from the waterfall,
I swear, you have never left my mind
The beak of the green parrot sank deep into the river
The one who guarantees happiness has left in a time of grief.

Perhaps someone had been singing earlier, but I hadn't noticed it because I was so absorbed in my work. Or maybe the singing seemed suddenly louder in the deep stillness of the night. Sometimes the sound was loud and melodic, and at other times it slowed into a dirge, as if somebody were wailing in grief. I stood up. Drawing a shawl around me, I came out and stood on the verandah. Because of the tension of the coming day's work, sleep wasn't reaching out to me. The fog spread everywhere, and the trees dripped with moisture. There was one bulb shining on the verandah and it seemed to tremble with the cold. I suddenly remembered a saying I had heard somewhere, that military men weep at night. Perhaps I had heard it from mother in my childhood. The voice in song returned. The soldiers' room was right in front of me, and the song was clear:

> *In the smoke of the cars,*
> *My fate has been burned;*
> *you can pick through my remains, my love.*

Then, after some time, the voice slowed and turned again into a kind of wail.

We were completely overwhelmed with our work the next day. There wasn't a minute to exchange a word with anyone. There was so much fog in the morning that the staff who came from outside arrived late, and it took some time to set things right and get everyone in order. By seven o'clock, the officers began to make themselves felt. The casting of votes didn't start on time, so we and the soldiers were reprimanded by the higher-ups: the soldiers were reprimanded by the military officers and we by our own. It was a separate matter entirely that not a single voter had turned out to cast a vote in the cold. I was in charge of the civilian staff, so I was lost in my work the whole day. Once in a while I came across him, but I rushed past. He complained: "You can't even look in my direction today. Very busy."

We were finally free around seven or eight o'clock that night. The official truck was supposed to pick us up, but it didn't arrive on time. We were exhausted from waiting. Winter was at its peak, and the cold climbed up slowly from below. There was so much fog that water dripped from the trees as if it were raining.

In the end we entreated the watchman to bring something from the village to burn. After casting the vote, the whole village had disappeared as if they had lost all interest in us. The Havaldar went with the watchman and brought back a sack of dried cow dung cakes and everything we needed to make tea. The watchman also gathered wood from here and there, and soon we were sitting in the courtyard before a roaring fire. All of us were dead tired. God bless that watchman who kept serving us tea. It helped us to bear cold. The Havaldar started telling tales of his service in military. The remaining three military men would look carefully at the Havaldar before speaking, as if they were shy of speaking before him. Perhaps they were forbidden to mix too much with civilians.

Otherwise they were quite open with each other and would tease each other by calling each other "sentry." It seemed to be some kind of joke among them. One of us would doze off from time to time from exhaustion and then, when the circle of tea would pass, would try to force our eyes open and listen to the conversation. The others would laugh out loud at watching the distorted faces struggling to listen.

I asked, "Who was singing that song last night? I want to hear it again." All three military men looked at the

Havaldar and smiled, as if sharing a secret. Perhaps the Havaldar was fond of chatting, because he said: "Tell your story, Sahib; we can hear the song later on."

One of the soldiers came forward quickly and started to speak: "Okay, I'll tell you my story." Before beginning, he looked at the Havaldar; he too was now ready to listen. He loosened his uniform so that the time could pass in comfort. We had all done our duty. We were exhausted, but we were also relaxed.

The soldier's eyes shone in the flames of fire, and he began to move his dry, cracked lips.

"A new sentry entered our unit. He cried all night long. Maybe he always did that, we thought. Who knows? No one could figure out what the crying was all about. His officers were shocked. There was a lot of guesswork, trying to come up with an answer. But how? No one had a clue. If the officers asked him to take a leave from the army, he would say no. When he was asked if he needed money, he would refuse that too. If he was asked whether he was forced by his father to join the army, he would not respond. Then the officers gave me the task of figuring it out. We lived in the same barracks.

"So it was my job to stick to him and conduct my investigation. The officers said that if I could figure out the cause of his sickness, I would be rewarded with one month's salary and one month's leave. You know, we army men long for home all the time. It is a tough job, being far away. I was supposed to find the truth within ten days and make my report to the officers.

"Almost nine days passed, and I still had no clue, not even an inkling. I stayed awake all night, spying on him. Wherever he would go, I would tag along. I tried to trap him into talking about it, but he wouldn't give up anything.

"It was on the last day that I received a letter addressed to me. I opened it and read it, but I couldn't make head or tail of it. It was a strange letter and it wasn't signed. It was written in red ink. I read it again and again. Finally, I showed it to the new sentry. He had been lying with his face down into the bed. When he saw the letter, he began to kiss it and then suddenly to weep. He said: 'This is my mine! This is my letter! I had given your name because I couldn't receive a letter in my own name.' I begged him again to tell me what it was all about and finally he unfolded the whole thing before me.

"'I love a girl and she also loves me,' he told me. 'This is her letter. She used to write to me in my other unit through another person, but I couldn't get her letters here until now. We both want to get married but our parents won't allow it. Then my father had me enlisted in the army. Now she writes to me in blood, and I do the same.'

"My job was done. I had figured it out. The next day, I told everything to the officers. They asked me what I could do. They said instead of going home, I should do something for my friend—they would give me the leave they had promised me. They also gave me the money. So I decided to go home later, and to do something for the sentry first. I went to his house and told his parents: 'Your boy has fallen in love with a girl.'

"The parents said, 'We know.'

"I said, 'Then why don't you let them get married?'

"They said that they had no objection, but the girl's parents have to agree too, don't they? The next day I went to the house of the girl's parents and told them my whole story and asked for the hand of the girl for my friend. In the end they agreed. And so he got married.

"After getting married, my friend asked me if there was any thing he could do for me. 'Do you have any problems?' he asked. I said that actually, I had the same problem he had. I love a girl and her parents won't allow us to marry. So he went to meet girl's parents, just as I had done. But this girl's mother would not relent. And that's how it remains. Now we have both decided that we won't get married at all. So far she has not married, and neither have I."

His story was finished. While telling the story, he had not looked at the Havaldar even once. The Havaldar sat to one side, his face bent down. It seemed as if the other soldiers already knew the story, so it was only new for us. The story had silenced everyone as they sat listening. When it ended, a smile spread across some faces. Some who had been sitting uncomfortably tried to make some kind of joke out of it. The soldier got annoyed.

"How could any of you understand, if you haven't truly loved another? There is no blood left in the cheeks of someone who is truly in love. He can't feel hunger or thirst. Can't eat, can't sleep." He spoke, looking me directly in the eye. I listened in silence.

One of the army men among them laughed and said: "Just look at his body. The name of that girl is written all over it." One of the other soldiers forcibly uncovered his back; there was her name. Now everything was about him and his love story.

After a long pause, someone said: "Do you still hope to be together?"

He said: "We are. Separation is a kind of unification; to remember someone is to be with them."

"If I were to abandon her memory, only then would I be apart from her. Recently we both were invited to a relative's house. I gestured to her to come to one side, and so we met, and I stood with my arms around her for a few moments. Her mother saw us from a distance. Our parents got together and said: 'Look at these two. How long has this game been going on?' Now it has become impossible for us to meet."

Someone asked: "What if the girl marries someone else?"

He said: "It is not possible. We will be together, if not now, then in in the future. We will live together or die alone. If we don't meet in this world, we will meet in next."

The truck that had been sent to fetch us finally came. Everyone ran towards it, forgetting the story. There was a huge rush. It must have been well past midnight. The truck was loaded with both soldiers and civilians.

The darkness was complete. People collided into each other. The back of the truck was filled with the election equipment and accessories. All the people crushed together in front of them. After a time, most people started to doze off. Whenever someone's head would droop in sleep and hit another person's face, or knock against the seat where another had found a perch, the other would wake up stuttering.

It reminded me of the black and white films of World War II soldiers returning tired and exhausted from the battlefront. The truck continued for such a long time in the black night. At last it stopped suddenly and there was a big commotion. This was where all the army men were supposed to get off. The journey for the rest of us had not yet ended.

Military trucks and jeeps stood outside in rows and the officers were giving instructions to the young men. The intense darkness surrounded us outside as well as inside. The truck was quite old, and its drivers were annoyed because they had been forced into doing this work for the government. The military men woke up and rushed to pass their bedding and other things quickly out of the truck. In the middle of the rush, the Havaldar appeared before me from somewhere to shake my hand and say good-bye.

I was sitting near the window, peering into the darkness. I was looking for him, the soldier who had told the story. I don't know why. At last, the soldiers had unloaded all their luggage and the driver moved the truck forward slowly. One army man had lost his helmet and because of this he was climbing up and down from the truck repeatedly. If he couldn't find his helmet, he would be punished. The poor man was exasperated, climbing on and off, again and again, his friends taunting him. At last he found his helmet—who knows how?—and the truck could move on.

Finally, I saw him. He was standing just a few steps from my window, looking towards me for who knows how long. His eyes were shining in the dark and there was a childlike smile on his face. Our eyes met and, for a moment, were one.

Rain

IT KEEPS ON raining, and I still sit in front of the window. Water pours down from the rooftops, balconies, parapets, and walls, and spills out of the gutter pipes. Cascading and falling, it moves without stopping. Our street gets a good cleaning: the torrent carries away soil, mud, straw, and rubbish. It must have risen up waist-high in the main bazaar, and the neighbourhood boys must be taking a dip, jumping in and out, splashing water on each other. Ashraf Sahib, who lives in the big yellow house, says bathing in this filthy water gives people sores and pimples, but Hanifa the ice vendor says it cures them.

But aren't these all tales of times long gone by? Water doesn't collect in the main bazaar any more and the boys don't bathe there. They laid new sewer pipes there because our old neighbourhood fell into the constituency of the Prime Minister.

Soil-coloured water, mixed with mud and straw, comes down through the gutters of our house and our rooftop is withering away. I am worried. We'll have to fix it when the time comes. Our family will be put to work and Auntie will braid her hair in two plaits, relaxing on her colourful bed without a care, watching us work.

I'll have to carry a sack of straw on the back of my bicycle. If I straighten the bicycle, the sack will tilt over; when I fix the sack, then the bicycle won't be straight. Later I'll also have to fetch cow dung in the container from Asghar, the Gujjar. As always, he will load up the container more than I can handle and dare me to carry it. I won't be able to lift it. The owner of the bullock cart will bring three cartloads of soil and unload them in the street. After mixing cow dung and straw with the clay and making a hollow for water in the middle, we will put on shorts to jump and dance in the wet clay and forget everything. From a crack in the window Auntie will behold the spectacle.

My mother and elder sister will plaster the whole roof. Auntie will warm herself in the winter sunshine after having spread her cot on the clean, new rooftop and will fix her hair again in two long braids.

72

After I grew up, Auntie didn't try to get me to do things anymore. But my younger brothers, Chaachi and Kaachi, they still had to take care of everything. But then Kaachi went overseas long ago. Auntie could not have ever imagined that Kaachi would one day go off to a foreign country. To the country of whites, of all places! But now Auntie's two sons have also gone away to America. She has settled there herself. Many people have asked me why Auntie stopped trying to get me to do things for her; she didn't even talk with me. Hate, you see, is something you have to feed and care for, just as love is. I harboured a seventeen-year-long hatred for Uncle and Auntie.

After my father's death we had no choice but to live with our uncle. I nourished my hatred and it burned deep and fierce within me. I'll tell it how it was: I never once quarrelled with Auntie, nor talked disrespectfully to her. All I did was look straight back into her eyes, silently. Auntie was fighting with Mother in the court-yard, and I stood by the window upstairs. The shadow of my silence must have fallen upon her. Irritated, she looked up. "What are you standing there for, ogling?" I had never met her eye before. In that quiet moment, I traversed backward on the path of a seventeen-year-old fear and didn't blink. When I did not waver, Auntie shook her head pompously and exclaimed, "Hunh," before she stormed into her room. How could she know how much my feet were shaking?

Ever since that day she didn't ask me to run her errands, and never spoke to me again. Thirty-five years have passed since then. The house has been sold and the old neighbourhood left behind. But the hatred has remained. Comrade Bali used to offer his advice. "Turn that hatred around and your sorrow will cease," he would say. "Look at your Auntie with love." Nice advice. Who knows how long Auntie is going to live? She is alive and well and looks better and better each time she returns from America.

The rain keeps falling and I keep staring out the window. Right across is Sister Naseem's house and past the alley one can see their courtyard. Moments ago Sister Naseem's daughter (who's growing like a vine) went downstairs after collecting the clothes that were hung up to dry on the rooftop. Her mother follows closely behind her. She knows that I stand in the window. She senses it every time; it is her daughter who is oblivious. A while back I was taking a leak in front of the door of our house. As I was tying the cord of my trousers, Sister Naseem happened to appear within the frame of her door. Her nostrils fluttering, she said, "You are old enough for solid food, little boy! Relieve yourself inside!"

Dumbstruck, I kept staring and blinking at her. Sister Naseem's eyes are so huge. And so dark. Her husband's been in some Arab country for many years now. Each time he comes, he leaves her with another child. As recently as two years ago she used to ask me to do her household shopping for her, but now she only gives me the look. But I don't look at her or at her soon-to-be grown-up girl. Their house just happens to be right

74

across from ours and one can look right into theirs. Besides, her daughter doesn't look at anyone, though everyone looks at her. All she likes to do is to look at a mirror. And the mirror looks at her. Both the mother and the daughter have such long hair. Sister Naseem's father-in-law sits on the verandah every Sunday and dyes his hair black or washes his old bicycle. Every other month or so he buys a small packet of black colour and paints his bicycle. It is too high for him. Who knows how old it is! The neighbourhood boys tease him, saying *"Pehli vaddi laam di eh"*—That bicycle is straight out of the First World War. I have heard he was married three times, but now no one is around.

I have no idea where Sister Naseem's gone. They left the house so abruptly. I heard that they had rented the place out and that there was a case against them pending in the court. Who are the new tenants?

The rain keeps pouring down and I sit by the window. The water will collect in front of Sister Naseem's house, and outside Sharif's general store. The open space belonging to the Gujjars will fill up too and they will have to milk their water buffaloes out in the alley. Auntie's courtyard will turn into a pond and the frogs will croak all night. People say that Auntie Maasi's husband became a fakir, or holy man. Some say they have seen him begging at such and-such place. A few say he's taken to getting high and wastes his life away at various shrines. I have not seen him myself. There are some plants and *dhrek* and guava trees in Auntie's courtyard.

She has taken to raising chickens and survives by selling eggs.

Baba Sharif has put bricks down at intervals on the street in front of his store. The children will reach his store hip-hopping and jumping from brick to brick and playing with the water, but if Uncle Jameel Sahib goes to the shop he won't be able to make himself jump from one brick to another. Watching him, the children wait for a bit. Then they forge ahead, splashing in the water, drenching him for sure. This invites his curse: "Bastard puppies, devil's children, I have yet to offer my *Maghrib* evening prayers!" Rain or shine, he has to go to the mosque with his old umbrella. It is from the British time and is patched up all over. Why doesn't Sister Naseem's father-in-law give up his bicycle, and Uncle Jamil Sahib his umbrella?

The rain pours down and I know that Sonia and her younger sister must be bathing on the rooftop next to ours. But what excuse can I use to go to our rooftop? We have already brought our cots downstairs and God forbid, if her sister Bushra catches even a whiff of me she's going to kick up a storm. Anyway, what can one do about Sonia? If only she could stick to one person! Anyone who has a bit of money, a few pairs of pants, keeps himself clean and spiffy, and wears dark glasses can command her attention. Now look at Bushra. She wouldn't give anyone the time of her day before she got married. She too was attractive. Kashmiris usually are. How keen she was to get married! She got married all right, just as she wanted to, but didn't stick it out. Six months into the marriage, she was back, and he never came to get her. She was loose lipped from the start. Now she quarrels all day long. She quarrels with every vendor who ventures to our alley and makes trouble with shopkeepers at the bazaar. They are our neighours; we share a wall. Whenever I went to their house in the hot weather, I'd find their mother with a wet scarf covering her shirtless torso. The boys of the neighourhood claim that the grown-up brothers and sisters of the house change their clothes in front of each other without any inhibition. I often wish, with God's grace, that someone would tell Bushra that she's still good-looking. She manages the entire household, but she creates friction with everyone. She is so easily irritated; she quarrels, quarrels, and quarrels.

Who was it who said Bushra's gotten married again? I wonder how she is now. It's been so many years. I haven't had any news of her. I haven't been around their house either.

It is still pouring hard and Mrs. Kuwait, as I call her, comes running past our house. Her house is in the back of Sister Naseem's. She has only one son and he is in Kuwait. All alone in a huge house, without even a servant! She came from a village originally. Every once in a while a man or woman shows up at her door and leaves after few days. Mrs. Kuwait's only son is still unmarried. She's been on the hunt though for quite some time. Every year her son visits and returns without getting married.

There was a time when Ms. Kuwait's house was locked up—ever since the time the Hindus lived there—and the rumour was that it was haunted. Whenever loose kites fell on the roof during the festival of Basant, no one dared go after them. Then one day Mrs. Kuwait arrived on a *tonga* pulled by a bullock, and the house lit up. When she announced her son was in Kuwait and that she was looking for a bride, many mothers of young girls were very solicitous towards her. But when after three or four years her son didn't marry anyone, the mothers stopped speaking to her and started talking behind her back. Today I know Mrs. Kuwait will cook rice with brown sugar or deep-fried *puri* and bring some to our house, because she's friends with my mother. Every Thursday, in the early hours of the morning, they walk all the way to the shrine of Data Sahib, Lahore's most famous shrine, wearing white *dupattas* and holding their edges between their teeth, counting on the rosary, "*Allah hoo, Allah hoo.*"

The son of Mrs. Kuwait kept coming for many years and then he left and didn't return. Many years have passed since she died, and I don't know who lives in their house now. The rain keeps coming down, keeps falling, and I am still perched by window . . . what else can I do?

To the right of Sister Naseem's stands Syed Ali Hyder Wasti's house. Hyder Wasti is in the same college as I am, but he hangs out with a different group. He's got two elder brothers and three elder sisters. His father is a scholar and has authored a few books. But he's been bedridden for the last few years. His wife keeps on feeding him medicine after medicine, year after year, but he doesn't get well. The elder sisters have studied up to university level and are working now. The brothers work too. In the beginning the sisters didn't like any of the prospective partners who came to meet them, and now no one comes pleading at their door. It seems as though the three sisters are angry with themselves, with time, with their brothers, with their parents, with everyone. The brothers say they won't marry as long as the sisters are not married. The sisters never come and stand by the windows, never watch the rain, or bathe on the verandah; they never talk with anyone. They always seem angry. All the brothers and sisters keep on working and working, getting older and older.

Syed Ali Hyder Wasti has now demolished the house and constructed a market instead, on the side where their walls touched the bazaar. But where are they themselves? There is no sign of them. I haven't met or even seen Hyder Wasti.

The rain still hasn't let up. I look out from the second storey window of my house, past Sister Naseem's house. Slightly to the left, at the end of the alley, I spot Riaz the postman sitting by the window of his house.

Riaz the postman has been retired for many years. He rents out the lower part of his house and lives in the upper two rooms all by himself. He built this house over fifteen, twenty years by gathering bricks, one by one.

He would save his money bit by bit in the neighourhood committee and then spend it on his house.

People say his wife was stunning: aquiline nose, dark skin, medium height and a shapely behind. She ran away with Khursheed, taking all four of her children with her. That is not the complete truth. She did run away with Khursheed, but she didn't stay with him. She only used Khursheed to reach her old love. Khursheed was a rickshaw driver. One day when Riaz was at work, Khursheed entered the house without knocking. People heard Riaz's wife yelling and then saw Khursheed running out of the house. Khursheed was quite tall and strongly built. No one had the courage to stop him. This episode repeated itself a few days later. Gradually, Khursheed would enter Riaz's house in broad daylight, but his wife wouldn't say a word. Riaz found out and beat her up. People could hear the children crying all through the neighourhood. After that, she walked off with Khursheed one day. She gathered her children, prepared a couple of bundles, gathered up all the money and gold, and left in Khursheed's rickshaw, never to return. The old men of the neighourhood still recollect all they saw and take pleasure in remembering her beauty.

Khursheed reappeared a few days later. Riaz had filed a case against him at the police station, but they let him go the same night. He explained that she had left him, too, for someone she knew before she married, and had settled in Karachi. A few days after the wife's disappearance, Riaz started to cry, thinking of her and the children. Later he tried to get married many times, but the matchmakers only milked him, and he remained unmarried. He's been such a simpleton all his life.

As a postman, Riaz knows everyone and everything in the old neighourhood. He retired after forty years of service. Since our government started changing the names of the roads, neighourhoods, alleys and all, Riaz has found new work. He's the only one who knows the old names. On top of that, he knows each and every person, in every house. Even other postmen come to him for help regarding letters with old addresses like "Arjun Road, Shivaji Street, Krishna Alley." Now Riaz lives alone and cooks his own food. Whenever we see him he's got some problem or other, or he's ill. It appears as if he exists outside time: it doesn't go forward for him, nor does it shrink. He steps outside of time and watches it pass by him. And he just keeps on watching. Quietly sitting for many years now, he watches. He gazes at the boys playing carrom on a board, monkeys playing, the kite fights during the festival of Basant, watching people walking out from the alleys, the rain: he just keeps on watching and watching.

The rain has let up a bit and the newly washed and cleaned coal-tarred road shimmers in the silvery evening.

It would be great if Zafari showed up. He's got to have a packet of cigarettes with him.

All the friends will gather at Boota Tea Stall and as usual we'll return home late into the night. It is the end of the month of Bhadon, around mid-September. Amjad Sahib has put on his crumpled, half-sleeve sweater even before the winter has set in and is now dodging water puddles on his way to get milk, holding a container.

It would have been nice if Zafari had come. He lives a few lanes from here. Shouldn't I go and find him? But his father will say he's not at home. He'll deliver a few taunts as well.

Soon the night, black like Sister Naseem's huge, dark eyes, will be here. A cool breeze will blow at night; the hazy moonlight, sneaking in through doors and windows, will make visible the slithering snakes that the breeze creates on puddles in the street. The colours seen through the window at night never pale in the unconscious mind: the colours of the night, rain, and evening. Only the silence is thick and deep in the pale light of the alley's streetlamp. The light of Syed Ali Hyder Wasti's house will remain on for a long time, and the sweet sound of voices will waft our way from Bushra's house. Many will glue their ears to Riaz the postman's radio that is playing old Hindustani songs.

I'll be sipping my tea with friends at the tea stall, and Taqi and the Professor will bore everyone by getting stuck in an argument on some worthless issue. I'll be thinking of Gulabo. Rain or no rain, I'm left standing by the open window. The lovely thing is that Gulabo lives downstairs, and water doesn't gather in front of her house.

You'll ask why I haven't said a word about Gulabo. What can I say to you about Gulabo? Who knows where she is now?

Sweater

MY MOTHER TOLD ME that she had knitted this sweater the same year that Abbi, my father, breathed his last in the hospital, owing to the doctors' negligence. For the rest of her life, Mother insisted that my father would not have died if doctors had not injected him with the wrong medicine.

I don't mean to talk about them, though; this story is about a sweater.

Father died in the month of Poh, in late December or early January. Before that he had been bedridden for a couple of months. The poor man was not lucky enough to make it to winter, let alone enjoy wearing his new sweater. Mother had knitted it that year with great fondness. We were small at the time, but we all remember that each time Mother recalled our father over the years, she would add: "I knitted that sweater with so much affection, but your father didn't have the chance to use it. He wore it only once when we went to the bazaar on a tonga. We ate fresh coconut and bought flannel cloth for you all."

After Father passed away, some of his clothes were given away, and some were saved for us children for when we would be ready for them. The sweater was taken by our youngest paternal uncle, who was a student then, and who also had been close to my father. There used to be very little clutter in the house. Whatever things there were, we all knew their history; now my hair is turning grey, but I can still remember it all. After Father passed away, Mother brought some household items that had been stored in the house of our other uncle since Partition: a big brass *praat*, for holding dough, the headboard, sidebars, and posters of a good-sized bed, a large brass platter, and two huge and very old chairs.

Mother remembered the story of each and every thing. "This brass *praat* was bought by your Mama, my brother, from Mr. Dhariwal," she told us. "This big bed frame was made under the watchful eyes of your grandfather, who supervised the carpenter personally while sitting in the courtyard. The carpenter was paid for his labour with some sugar and wheat." We brought the bed into the house, but we had no space for it. There was only one room for all of us. Later, the bed was assembled and then pushed and prodded into the room. Mother sometimes saved old trunks and things under it. We three brothers slept on that bed for many years. Within just a few months, the cotton webbing stretched across the wooden frame loosened and began to fall apart. Often we would go to sleep on the bed at night only to wake up on the floor in the morning.

But this story is about the sweater. Mother remembered it, too, for many years.

Mother was in the habit of relating her dreams each and every morning. She would tell me: "I saw your Abbi in my dream last night. He was wearing white clothes, and he was looking at me with a smile. He was wearing that sweater."

My youngest uncle became a big official after completing his studies, and once he got married, we didn't see him much. But he would come to visit us once or twice a year, and each time before leaving, he would caress our hair, sigh heavily, and hand something to Mother. For many years, our uncle's one or two visits were all we had to look forward to. When I passed the tenth-grade exams with high marks, our uncle came to meet us, and he suggested that I go on for higher studies. For many years, the other uncles had been saying that we should be sent to work. When leaving, my aunt gave us some used clothes, and among them was

Mother's knitted sweater. When I wore the sweater that day, Mother went quietly into the other room. We knew this habit of hers.

After my graduation, a different kind of bird began to fly in me. I didn't know much about it except that its flight was to the west. With a friend I headed towards Afghanistan, then through Turkey, Bulgaria, and Belgrade, and finally we reached Italy by train. I became like a tree there, a tree without a sparrow in its branches, without earth to settle into. No one offers a thing when you arrive in such a place. How can one earn a living, with nothing to begin with? And then there is the problem of finding work at all. When we ran out of money, we had to live on the street. Then the winter hit. Those who had not experienced the winter over there had no idea. The underground tunnels where the Metro trains run, they became our last resort, the only place left that could keep us warm. There we found many who were exiles in their own country: the old men, drunken women, the boys who had fled from work or were without work—they could be found among the dark boys from our poor countries.

And then the police would come and force us to leave, and we would stand out on the road in the piercing cold night. I was wearing the same sweater then. That, two more, and then a fat jacket over them. But no way, this was not the winter of our country. This winter was foreign, and the slaying air was something we could not know. One morning, after staying awake all night at the station, I was freshening up at a public toilet. We could have a free meal at a church if we got there in time. If late, we would have to starve for the day. So I was in a hurry and left my sweater hanging in the toilet. After I ate, I realized it was missing and ran back for it. The sweater was still hanging there, waiting for me, two hours later.

When I did find work, I was overwhelmed by strange memories of my country. One dream in particular came to me many times, like a painted still life: An empty room with a table and some chairs, some crockery, and half-eaten food on the table. Nobody sat in the chairs. It was as if someone had just gotten up from there a moment before and left it all behind. In the dream, I try to reach inside but cannot. I am hungry, and I want to eat my fill. But I cannot. I had not realized that I would never be able to live to my satisfaction without being with my own people.

Memories would descend on me, and my eyes would be soaked in tears. I would remember the air on Lahore's Mall Road, and the city's old trees. The empty crate for bottles at Fajjy's Coffee House, which we used to sit on when we went to drink tea. The water standing in the deserted lanes of Krishan Nagar, where I grew up, in the evenings after the rains, with snakes moving through the water. The weak streetlights, and the dim lights filtering out of silent homes.

After a year and a half, I came back to my country like a man without spirit, shivering with cold. I was wearing the sweater again. Mother said: "You have come back the same person as when you went away." After a long and hard struggle, I was able to complete my education, and begin my career. With time, more was added to it.

Some time back, one of Mother's relatives came to visit her. She used to live in another city, but her husband had just retired. When she went away, mother told me that she had come to see me, looking for a job for her eldest son. They were living well until her husband retired, but it seemed that they had nothing to live on since. It was difficult for them even to keep a roof over their heads. She kept talking to Mother in a low voice, and I saw that her eyes were sad.

When the woman was leaving, Mother gave her some old clothes and that sweater was among them. By now, it was worn out. It was hard to say if it could even be worn. The wool was full of snags, and the shoulders were all stretched out. It had a strange and clumsy appearance. I said: "Mother, a thing should be in good shape to be given away. How can anyone wear that?" But the woman quickly picked it up and dropped it back with the other clothes, saying: "It can be worn under a shirt. Besides, handmade sweaters have a warmth of their own."

Unstory

THIS IS NOT a story. It cannot be said.

This is just the rumbling of my memories.

It is a voice that swims and swims in the underworld of my unconscious. After remaining ensnared in the preoccupations of the day, it emerges after midnight, speaking in the quiet darkness.

Someone is hitting the electricity pole with a brick.

I had nothing but free time after I passed the grade 10 exams. I read detective novels from the neighbourhood's penny library—one anna per book. On summer nights, I would light the table lamp on the roof, cover it with newspaper so that the light would not leak out, and read detective novels through the night. The distance between reading and not reading was finally exhausted after midnight. I became a spy from those detective novels and began my investigations in my dreams. During the day, I would watch people with suspicious eyes. Then, after some days, something odd happened. The worlds of novel and rooftop merged, and the spy came out of the book.

Someone struck the electricity pole a few times in the middle of the night.

I was frightened at first. Should I get up from bed or not? Should I turn off the table lamp and watch, or pull the sheet over on my head and forget it all? No. A shadow came from the house of the family of weavers in front of our house and went a bit further down the street. Then it was lost in a plot overgrown with dry and wild *aak* plants.

This became routine. Late at night, somebody would bang the electricity pole two or three times. With hesitation. And then after a long silence, a shadow would appear from among the weavers' houses and disappear again.

What should I do? If I were from one of Ibn Safi's famous novels, what would I do? What would I do, if I were his main character, Captain Imran? Investigate: that would be my mission.

There was a row of ten or so small, connected houses in the *mohallah*. People called them the "weavers' houses."

Most had only one or two rooms. From our rooftop we could easily see into their courtyard. Children would run from here to there, across it. The women would sit in the sun, searching for lice in the children's hair. There were handlooms in a couple of the rooms that were separate from the houses.

The men wove cloth all day long. Whenever we could manage to look inside the rooms, we would watch the cloth appear, woven out of skeins of many-coloured threads. Rehemta and his father would grab and pull the cloth in their hands, stretching it from side to side. The clatter of the handloom echoed through the houses in the neighbourhood, swimming through our minds.

Not a single girl from the weavers' houses was considered beautiful. They did not go to school; they didn't worry about adorning themselves in the name of fashion. Their noses flowed, and they would peek outside through tattered mats hanging on the doors of broken-down homes. I used to look over at their houses from our house above, but my eyes never lighted on anyone's face. Sometimes it appeared as though someone there was looking back at me from some of the houses' empty roofs.

But no, that's not true. Mani was from one of those houses. Married or not, anyone would sigh upon seeing her. When she passed by on the street, it seemed as if she had crushed our hearts under her feet on her way. The boys would say: "She passes by, and everything hurts." Everyone said, "She is the red in the colourful cloth of the fakirs." Her body made waves that passed through everyone; when she had walked by, hearts would empty.

I became a spy. And I got a hint of something.

But my heart could not accept it. No, it can't be. I must have misunderstood. What had I seen with my own eyes, anyway? Still, love and its scent can't be hidden.

Bali used to drive a bicycle rickshaw. He was six feet tall, with deep black skin and red eyes. He would twist his thick moustache and oil would drip from his forehead. But it couldn't be.

I started to watch ahead of time, in anticipation of the sound from the electricity pole. The man would come from one side. The long shadow and walk were the same.

Mani's marriage was arranged by her parents. The husband would have been good enough, poor guy. But only God knows how things work with the heart. Even after the wedding she didn't leave it. She ended up coming back with her two children. Bali took them all in. No one knows if there was actually a divorce or not, but Bali became the father of those two children and two or three more of their own.

They were a strange couple. Bali would come back in the evening with his rickshaw and take his rowdy gang of children to the bazaar for entertainment. They would stand outside and eat junk food there. They didn't exhibit an ounce of shame or concern for what anyone thought. Women are supposed to feel the sting of shame, they say, but she behaved as if it was nothing. "Thank God, the witch has left us," the others would say about her. And the men's sighs were left in their hearts.

Bali did win his *Heer*, his beloved. But her story was reduced to rubble in the dust of the streets. The rickshaw didn't bring in much money, and Mani's beauty became tarnished. She had left the well-provisioned house of her first husband for her "dark ghost" who came in the night. She didn't make a single complaint.

I still remember when the first procession against the Ayub government started from our neighbourhood, Krishan Nagar, and Bali was at the head of it. At the time, a huge billboard advertising the latest movie stood in front of Khoti High School, at the back of the Laat Sahib's office, where the Chief Minister sat. That was the first thing to be broken down and turned into sticks. And then it was a free-for-all on Mall Road. The boards were set on fire and the painted faces of the actors burned and became ash. Then the tin used for the background was converted into doors and windows for houses. One of them remained as the door of Bali's house for a long time.

He became a leader of the People's Party, an unpaid worker who helped other people to gain office. Was there anyone in the neighbourhood to whom he hadn't shown that photo of his, the one of him with Zulkifar Bhutto? That photo hung in Hanifa's shop for many years.

The People's Party did come to power, but what was there in it for him? He was neither literate nor educated.

Though his influence was everywhere, his place was the same. Sometimes he was able to help people who came to him, and sometimes not. He became tense and irritated. The leaders started avoiding him.

He kept driving the rickshaw. Mani was unrecognizable after giving birth to so many children. Bali started taking drugs. Their relationship remained close and warm, but, outside, the world was cold. When Bhutto was hanged, Bali was the first to be arrested. Just like that. He had done nothing. He hadn't even acknowledged Bhutto's death. The Islamists must have been watching him.

By the time he came out of prison, Bali had fallen fully into the hands of the addicts. He slowly transformed into a skeleton. He couldn't even drive the rickshaw anymore. Mani also became weaker and weaker.

The boys were given as bonded labour to shops. Time dissolved like intoxication. The houses became bigger, and streets became narrower. But Bali's house was the same. The same old rough cloth over the tin door. Tall houses were built all around them, their tiny house folded in tight among them.

I went to visit my old *mohallah* recently and someone mentioned Mani. Is she alive? Maybe. After Bali's death, the boys had sold the house and started their own small business. Until the end, Mani didn't want to leave the house. For several years after the house was sold, she could be seen wandering like a shadow in the neighbourhood. Now there is a three-storey house standing where Bali's house once was. Is she still alive? Perhaps. The handlooms are all gone now, and houses built in their stead. The boys are educated now and working in offices.

The visit to the *mohallah* had been forced on me. My younger brother's first wife had passed on, and he had begged Rehmata's wife to make a match for him. At last she sent a message that she had found someone for him. When I went to meet her on his behalf, I was shocked at how old she had become. While talking, I asked her about Mani, and just like that a shadow of remembrance passed over her face. She said that they had sold their house and left, who knows where they went, it was so many years ago.

Mani?

I don't know.

But this is not a story. It is the sound of an electricity pole being struck at midnight.

The Estranged City

THE CITY OF Lahore continues to change. Familiar things have gone missing, and its strangeness is everywhere. Places are something different, and so are the people. But a few old corners are just the same. They are un-changing, and they fill one's heart with memories.

Lahore's Mall Road is one of those places. Childhood makes memories, youth fills it with colour, and age brings regret. One might travel one's whole life the distance from Appha's tea stall to Gol Bagh, the "round garden" where all the famous public political meetings took place, but that path will never end. Jeejj would go from Gol Bagh to Alfalah at Charing Cross by foot, maybe three kilometers, drenched in rain. When depression struck him, Yousafi would wear fine clothes and go to the airport from his home on Dev Samaj Road on a bicycle. Now that road goes by an Islamic name. Upon his return, we would meet him somewhere on Mall Road. Jeejj would tell us that he wasn't able to smoke cigarettes while taking his bath in the rain.

There used to be two coffee houses in Tollinton Market, the Capri and the Kabana. There were also small huts behind the market. If someone wanted to sit and have a quick drink, in private, that was the place. Some friends would sit in those coffee houses all day long. If you went there, you could meet them. Some you might meet at the old Anarkali Bazaar. Others you'd meet just standing on the road. Now there is nothing: neither the Tollinton Market, the coffee houses, nor the people.

That day I was coming on foot from the main post office to Gol Bagh. Peeju used to set up his stall there, opposite the YMCA. He had a tiny place on the ground floor, with the same on the upper floor. You could squeeze three or four tables in on the bottom, and the same above. People all sought to sit on the upper floor, to sit at the window and watch the flow of the city's traffic on Mall Road. Sitting near the window and watching the rains outside, it was as if one were sitting in some Parisian café.

Lahore in the mid-1970s was nothing like it is today. Evening would wander in slowly and descend softly on the edges of the heart. All that matters in youth is friendship; there is nothing more. Peeju's was an expensive place, and we were from poor families. If any of us disadvantaged types happened to see anyone we knew sitting as we passed in front of Peeju's, we would rush in. Our friend Karm would pause, but others would quickly climb the stairs shamelessly. Then it would be time to offer tea to both the shameless and the ashamed. They would be there already, to find cigarettes. The boy from the rich Memon family, who used to live in Rang Mahal, would always sit at Peeju's. There is no trace of him now. Wahid Malaal had made good use of him. Who knows what he whispered in his ear, but he avoided us. Wahid was just like us but made as if he were different. As if he knew so much more.

This was a time when so many were caught up in the idea of revolution. But those who gathered at the YMCA and the tea stalls mostly wanted to be writers. There was an unbridled passion for reading and writing. Many had read about different philosophies from around the world—they fought and dismissed everything, all in one piece. Some would sit with us, just like that, and we had no idea what they were doing there. Then they would suddenly disappear. It was a strange party: old political rabble-rousers, failed lovers, radical intellectuals spouting new ideas and methods, disheartened political workers, literary one-hit wonders who could boast of writing just one or two decent things, journalists, famous columnists, well-known writers, bored college and university students, with a few women among them. We were all newcomers. Any one of us would start telling his or her story, and we would understand part of it, but not all. But we had all written something or other. Then we were all quickly scattered, and everything disappeared in the dust. Most went back to complete their studies. They pushed and manoeuvred, used their wits, made the most of the opportunities that came their way, sat for competitive exams—and so they made a place for themselves, big or small. They built houses in the fanciest neighbourhood in the city, in Defence, and married into good families. Now they recall those long-gone days with a sigh. Those like me were devoured in the struggle just to make ends meet. We fought with time itself.

I passed through the square past where Peeju's coffee house used to be and kept walking straight. Appha's tea stall used to be there too, on the corner on the left. The place had now been taken over by a shop selling ready-made children's clothing. Appha fought in court to hang onto it, but it must be thirty or thirty-five years now since he lost the case. I kept walking, slowly. The jewellers' shops were on my left and, in the old days, the BRB Library, Peeju's, and Cheeny's Restaurant would have been on my right. All of them are gone now, except the jewellers' shops. They now survive only in books. A mosque was built on the green strip of land along the footpath, where addicts congregated to sleep. Many green patches of land along the roads were converted into mosques in the 1980s during Zia-ul-Haq's reign. This was one.

I had entered Tollinton Square, where the Market used to be, and stood there. There was now a juice stall on the left, where there used to be only grass and benches. Tables and chairs were arranged there. Boys and girls from the nearby art college were coming and going from the stall, and I stood on the footpath. My car was in the parking lot behind the square. Shouldn't I too have a glass of juice? I thought. I had come to post books to some old friends from the main city post office.

I moved towards the chairs. He was on one of them, to the side, sitting apart. One leg was crossed over the other, and his body appeared wasted away. He wore a filthy pair of pants, a colourful checked shirt, a thick rope instead of belt, torn and dirty socks, and dusty boats with worn out laces. His face bore a rough shadow of stubble but seemed clean.

Our eyes met for an instant, and his gaze pierced me. I felt I had never seen such eyes before: familiar, knowing, hungry, longing to meet. Unwavering. As if a light had suddenly sparked in them, on a sleepless night, exhausted by years of waiting. It seemed like he had recognized me, and he seemed to smile inside. His gaze didn't falter.

"You . . . it's you."

Pain lingered on his face and appeared like a lost child. His eyes pulled me in.

"Has the world been conquered?" he said, with an almost wicked laugh. "You left me behind and kept running. Where have you got to? People like me were left to sleep on the road."

It was the last days of the spring month of Vaisakh, when the clouds would gather in the heat. But that day neither did the clouds prevail, nor did the sun show its face. The day got stuck somewhere in between. In the shadowy haze, the city flowed on. People were distracted from their work by the indeterminate weather, as if they were just waiting for the clouds, or as if they could only do their work if the sun appeared.

Then suddenly a sharp gust of dust-filled wind would come and circle before one's eyes, the colour of dreams.

He came into view like this piercing blast of air, like an artist's painting rendered in grey and drab colours.

"I have been searching for you all this time, but you had forgotten me. Remember how once when you were looking down from the roof of your house and, in your heart, you wanted to jump and die? When you were little, you used to go to your father's grave and weep. Oh God, lift me up. I couldn't bear it. I was with you. I am what is left of those dark times, the sighs of your hunger, the colour of your dry tears."

I was still standing on the footpath, and he sat on his chair. His eyes pierced me like the talons of a great bird, and I was struck by fear. Suddenly, the clouds descended, and it was as if night had fallen. The grass and trees became dark and thick. He appeared to me both very far away and very close. From the way he was sitting, it seemed as if he sat in that spot every day. He held himself comfortably, without any care in the world, with composure. No one looked at him, and not once did the waiter from the juice stall come over to him.

And so I remembered Munwar.

He was our distant relative. The son of my father's cousin. Punjab had just been divided. His father murdered his mother and was hanged. This all happened before we were old enough to know what was going on. The murder took place in our house in Krishan Nagar, near the Nori building. His father's shop was in Taxali, in the red light district, Heera Mandi, and there was some fight over a woman. He asked Munwar's mother to give him her jewellery, so that he could sell it. When she refused, he took a hatchet to her. The murder took place on the second floor, and the stream of blood flowed into the street. That's when the commotion began. Munwar had two sisters, but his uncle beat him, so he ran away from home and became an addict. One sister ran off with somebody. When she finally came home, she was married off to another man who already had many children. Many more came. Then her husband died. We heard her story but never saw her. For so many women, it is only their stories that remain.

People said Munwar would sit all day in front of the Laat Sahib's office, at the Punjab Secretariat. It had been built in British times. And there he was: blanket over his shoulders, with a long beard, naked feet, spit at the corners of his mouth, where dirt collected.

He used to come to our home from time to time. We took one look at him and were terrified. Worn out, dirty clothes, with a dirty beard. I was a child and would run to bring new soap and a razor. He would take a bath, shave, and my mother would give him some of my father's clothes. After my father passed away, she saved everything, and even I wore them after I grew up. After taking a bath, he would sit in the room with his legs crossed under his body and it seemed like he was totally normal. Then he would eat. God only knows how many rotis he would eat. He would keep on eating and my mother would keep on making them. When he at last had his fill, he would pat all the children's heads lovingly, murmur a prayer for us, and leave. When I started college, once or twice I saw him sitting in some corner near Laat Sahib, but I didn't dare to talk with him. From inside the blanket, his eyes moved across everything. All I could remember were those eyes.

And now they had a hold on me. I stood trembling on the sidewalk. The traffic on Mall Road kept moving. I set my face straight and crossed the square, quickly reaching the newly constructed Tollinton Market. I couldn't stop myself from looking back. His eyes appeared in front of me. "Go on, you didn't pay any heed to us nothings. It's not me alone: there are thousands, millions, billions like me. I have never left you. Below, beyond consciousness, I am there. Absent everywhere, present everywhere. Silent everywhere, hidden everywhere. From street to street, city to city, from country to country, at home and abroad too . . . Remember? I also met you in the underground Metro in Rome."

It happened forty years ago. I was shocked to see him. The Cold War had not actually ended yet, but the world was already changing. It was the last days of the Shah of Iran's regime. Boys from poor countries like ours were trying to enter Europe through Turkey's door. We travelled by road from Lahore and reached Rome within two weeks. We couldn't get a visa to go any further. When the money ran out, we were on the street. The day would pass somehow, but at night, it was cold. We would sleep underground, in the Metro. Hundreds of people slept there: people from the various countries of sub-Saharan Africa, from North Africa, and from Asia. At any one time, there would be people from at least thirty different countries. There were also some locals among them. We slept on flattened cardboard boxes that we found left outside the big shops after they closed.

Daytime prevailed in the middle of the night in the underground Metro stations. The Africans would wave bottles of booze around in their hands and talk loudly, sitting on the cardboard boxes. Everyone laughed and joked. The police would also show up to keep people in line. At that time, there was no prohibition on sleeping in parks and sidewalks in Europe, and we would stay in the underground to escape the cold. People would slowly find jobs and disappear, but then just as many others would appear. At night, a few people, who

seemed to be relatives, would come to visit the homeless and would give them food and bottles of liquor. Why
didn't they take them home with them? I'll never know.
Sometimes men even flirted with the filthy and drunken
middle-aged women in their midst—but then they
themselves were drunk, too. There would sometimes
be a younger woman in the group, who had somehow
become homeless. Many would flock to her side, but, in
her state, she had nothing to give them.

It was there that I met him. We had spread out our
cardboard boxes and were settling onto them. Shooky
was planning to go work on a ship. Hakeem Sahib
wanted to reach his brother in Germany. And then he
appeared from nowhere, wearing a long overcoat, with
a sweater underneath, his hair dishevelled. He was staggering from drunkenness. He made a full circle around
all the people lying on boxes and then stood before
us with great effort. It seemed like he would fall over,
any minute. He had a skinny body but sharp, piercing eyes. How come people like him all have such eyes?
Mohammad, the Egyptian, who slept near us, said suddenly, "A Pakistani." He overheard this and looked at us
sadly. I tried to recognize him. He could have been a boy
from any street of Lahore. The shadow of fear passed
over us. All of us had one question: were we all going to
become like this in time? He sat in front of us and took
a burger from the pocket of his overcoat. It was neatly
wrapped in brown paper. He placed the bottle of booze
before us. It was strong brandy, but we each took one

sip. This seemed to make him happy. We were so afraid of him—what strength did we have to say no?

After eating the burger, he picked up his bottle and got to his feet. He continued to look at us and then he came and stood right in front of me. He fixed his eyes on me as if we had some old connection. Who knows what he was looking for? He said something force-fully, and saliva spewed from his mouth. Mohammad, the Egyptian, gestured to me that he was asking me for money. I came forward to give him some Italian lira, saved somewhere in the corners of my pockets. He moved his hand emphatically, "Go, go away. You'll need it. Mothers weep when their sons leave. Go. The money will run out. Those who come here leave some-one standing at the door. Even the doors are worn out, waiting. Go away, go away, go away." Then, with anger about him he left, muttering, without taking any money, falling and staggering on his feet. He was tall and must have been handsome once. But all I remembered were his eyes. As if they were trying to look far into the dis-tance, and then suddenly were disappointed. As if he were looking closely at the path he had taken from Lahore, and it had now become a wall.

All eyes now gathered together in his eyes. Time passed and evening descended. Because of the day's hide-and-seek game of sun and clouds, the evening was a bit cool. For a moment it was as if everything had come to an end and stood still. The road emptied and then filled again. In the dark evening, he looked like a dot, and the glow of his eyes stopped me. He had full control, and I was caught by his eyes, imprisoned in his gaze. He looked like an insect under a bench, and I stood by.

Night had fallen. Who knows, was the old Anarkali group still sitting there, or had it come to an end? There were so many groups then. Back in those days there weren't so many carts selling things, so many clothes and shoe shops, so many eateries. There was the professors' group, the art college students' group, the students from the university dorms. Tea was served all night, a flood of words, mirth and laughter. Someone would get teased, and if it had an effect, the news would scatter through all the groups. But nobody ever got angry or left in anger. There was a leader of every group who would take care of everything and ask everyone to contribute money for tea at the end of the session. Some might not have even a penny to give, and another might pay for everyone. What mattered was who had said what, who was the most educated, and who was the wisest.

How long did I stand there? The rush of the traffic slowed. Where he was sitting, behind the trees, that was only the idea of him. He could not be seen in the dim light.

I shouldn't look back, I thought to myself. He will destroy me. I should look squarely ahead and go. The wind had slowly sharpened, and it was colder. The night helped the clouds to triumph and the air was damp. A sharp gust of air struck my face and blew up the dust. The air turned into wind, and with that the shopkeepers closed their shops, and the juice shop was deserted: only the plastic chairs and tables remained. I was able to see the old bodhi and peepal trees for the first time. How could they have survived the slaughtering of trees? Suddenly there was a blast, and the electricity went. The rain began to pound, and the cycles, motorcycles, and pedestrians disappeared. Only the cars crept along the road.

I looked towards him but couldn't see anything. There was pure darkness but for the soft glow of the flowing traffic, which would then disappear. People gathered under the newly built wood roof of Tollinton Market, waiting for a break in the rain. I started moving under the roof towards the garden. "Keep going, keep going," I said to myself. I knew that in just a few minutes I would reach the sidewalk on Mall Road, Gol Bagh, and the great Sufi saint Data Sahib's shrine. Then I would reach the place overflowing with addicts, day labourers, and poorly paid manual workers. I didn't look back and walked straight. Only my car was standing in the parking lot.

I started the car and drove along the road, towards the place where he had been. It was completely empty, pitch black, with the dim lights of cars slipping away. I didn't see him. When I passed where Peeju's café used to be, I heard the sound of weeping, and the sound of something falling. I stepped on the gas and kept on going.

The Door
Is Open

FIRST, the dream.

The same old house—our place in Krishan Nagar.

I wonder how long the dreams of that house will haunt me.

My tiny old room. It's the middle of the night. I have been reading Rajinder Singh Bedi's Urdu stories. All my life, I have loved them, though I always seem to get stuck on one line: "When we are with one friend, why do we still long for another?" I marvel at the beauty of the expression, the truth of this thing that Bedi has said. A sound intrudes from the street, and I go to the window. Three friends await me in the alley below. One of them stands in the moonlight; his face breaks into a smile upon seeing me. The other one is half in the moonlight and half in darkness. I recognize him too; he adjusts his glasses with his hand and clears his throat. The third one is completely obscured by darkness. I can only guess at who he is; but a guess, you know, is always just a guess. The first one, who is smiling, calls out suddenly in his thin voice: "Hey man, he came to see us, and we brought him here. Now he thinks we should go do something." I am still under the spell of Bedi's words: "When we are with one friend, why do we still long for another?" I, too, feel delighted to see him, that pleasure mixing with the sweet taste of Bedi's words. I say, "Come in." But wait. Let me sketch the entire map. I have been trapped in it all my life.

Imagine a house with two storeys. My uncle lived downstairs and we above. There were two rooms on the upper floor. Were you to enter the house through the main door, you'd pass through it and then to the right—no, to the left. Then you would find the stairs. The next thing is to climb up the ten steps—or perhaps it was more? Oh well, I went up and down those steps for twenty-one years, but now I seem to have forgotten. Let's say ten to twelve steps. (I'll ask Taqi. He's always going on about that house.) After going up, to your left, a door opened into a large room. Wait, I forget again. No, there were no windows or doors, just frames in the walls. We heard that after evicting us, my uncle repaired the house, adding doors and windows, and then sold it. My mother and brothers shared that room. Just a little further ahead, as the passage narrowed, there was a smaller room, also on the left. We referred to that room as the "gallery." My other uncle, if he heard me speak of it now, he'd be really amused. But, alas, he's not alive anymore.

That was my room. It was on the second floor, but it was still quite low and close to the street level. You could easily stand in the window and chat with a person down below.

Right next to the window there was a wall. That was the cause of all the trouble. At that time there was a lot beside the house. Although it was empty, it had four walls around it. (The lot isn't empty anymore; a three-storey building has now been built there.)

Everything I am describing is from that time when there was nothing there. Even the street itself has not remained as it was. And remember: we are talking of dreams here.

You could easily stand in the window and chat with someone standing down in the street.

I tell my friend, "Come up," and so he climbs the wall in a jiffy, balancing on the edge and moving across it. And then he's right there where I am. He hops in through the window and into my room. The two other friends are still standing at the door. The second one, half in darkness and half in light, adjusts his glasses and grumbles. He wants me to come down and open the door.

"I'm not scaling that wall and walking on that edge," he declares. I was afraid of doing it myself, had feared it all my life. Even now in my dreams it scares me. But who is going to open the door? I have already told you, my uncle lived downstairs.

We had lived under the tyranny of my uncle since childhood. We lived there, but we lived in fear. If we dropped something unintentionally, he'd roar from downstairs, "Can't you sit in peace, you dogs? Why are you making such a commotion? I gave you a place to live, now I have to put up with all your troublemaking, too!"

From childhood to adulthood, this fear climbed up the stairs to sit on top of us. It manifested itself in our bodies and breath, in our blood and brains, and in our souls. For twenty-one years he stood with his heel pressed down upon us. Dread left its enduring mark, while fear sculpted our lives. So, who's going to open the door?

I was the oldest among the brothers, so I inherited a bigger share. I have wrestled with it for the better part of my life. I have wanted to open the closed door. I am grown up now. The fear too has lessened. But it has not vanished completely. I don't know if my friends know this—the ones still standing in the street below, and the one who has climbed in, scaling the wall and walking across it.

The two friends remain standing at the door. I am afraid, and unsure of how to open the door. I remember Bedi's line again, "When we are with one friend, why do we still long for another?" Bedi could have spoken of a third friend as well. But Bedi never did. All of this belongs to the realm of dreams. When you cannot even open the door, why does he then insist on coming through? Why doesn't he simply climb the wall and walk across it, to come inside? Standing before him in the window, I invited him in a couple times. But he doesn't give me an answer. He is just like that. I know that he'll keep standing there, below, next to the door, for the rest of his life, and I by the window. The one who's already in says in his typical way, "Come on . . . What's your problem?" I stand next to window; the other one is still down there, beside the one who is engulfed by darkness, always hiding his body, always staying behind . . . Fear. No, no. I think of my uncle again and suddenly I feel it is nothing. I can go downstairs and open the door. It seems to me that the yearning to see friends is greater than fear. The yearning has overwhelmed the fear, and it is gone.

Suddenly I open my eyes. The crows are raising hell. The image of our old *mohallah* drifts past my eyes. It has been twenty-one years since we left that house and the neighourhood.

It's morning. A faint light has crept into the room through the window. It seems as though fear has climbed down the stairs and longing has climbed up instead, as if the twittering of sparrows has gradually overcome the crow's cawing. As I leave the room, I find the door has been left open. Why don't you come in?

Half Maghar Moon

IT WAS EVENING, halfway through the month of Maghar, as fall gave way to winter. The departing sun burned like a red ball among the dark rain clouds that gathered behind the shopping mall, which slithered like black cobras filled with poison. Clean, bright clouds could not keep their hold on the sky, as the departing redness of the sun bore holes through them with a biting winter wind.

But we poor folk, slowly dying in the city, thin and worn out, when did we ever have enough time to feast our eyes on this kind of show?

Perhaps it was on such a Maghar night, drenched in the seemingly cold but inwardly warm air, that one of my drunken poet friends had said, "My heart longs to kiss this wind." I could understand the literal meaning of his words, but not their full meaning. This is the season that the playwright Balwant Gargi called "pink season," sometime between summer and winter, with warm days and cool evenings.

But in my heart, the wind of another Maghar night was blowing.

I kept searching for the moon in the thick clouds, but the slices of cloud had become drunk, staggering and dissolving into the black night. Hidden within them were the drops of moisture carried by the cold winds of winter. The wind blew so hard that the clouds seemed to churn. This is the way the clouds of the middle of Maghar always are, unsettled and warm.

That old Maghar night smouldered on, like the moon. The clouds did their best to hide it away but were finally defeated and allowed it to shine through, letting it appear before us. This is one of those stories of my old home, in Krishan Nagar.

These thoughts of mine from thirty-five or forty years ago rise in the cold half Maghar night like a wind that continues to blow after the first rains of winter. The red sun of the last evenings of the month of Katak— I don't know why it pierces the heart so. Thoughts of the long nights of winter fill the heart, then empty it.

I was in eleventh class then, at the preparatory

college, and the pressure of the final year examinations for both the eleventh and twelfth classes was already upon us. I had gotten entangled in a strange situation that past summer and couldn't get out of it. We started college in April, and then during summer vacation, student elections had been held, and who knows how, but my meetings with the members of our Leftist group had increased. We were beaten up once or twice by the Islamists and participated in some demonstrations on Lahore's Mall Road. So we began to think a lot of ourselves. It was peak of the power of the People's Party government and student politics were hot. There was always something to keep us busy, something that would set fire, that would then smoulder among us.

I was barely seventeen or eighteen years old. I had just entered the college, and I was still under pressure to leave it and get a job. Our house was in Krishan Nagar, and we lived on the second floor. It had only two rooms, one big and one small. My room, where I lived and slept, was tiny, and it was a bit lower than the other room. My mother and my two brothers stayed in the big room. After my father passed away, we had come here to live in Lahore, and my uncle and his family lived on the ground floor.

Because of my associations with the Progressives, I started coming home late at night. My uncle made a scene about it for some time, but when he saw my budding facial hair, he kept quiet. He would say, "Sons, you have to study for yourself and not for me. This is the time—two, three years and, that's all. What you will earn for the rest of your life will be based on these years. These four years will count for forty years. Study, my sons, or else go find a job. I never went further than grade 10, but because of Partition, I got a good job. You won't get that so easily, I think."

But we were burning inside. After classes were finished for the day, there would be meetings in the college residence. There were discussions about new things happening, about new members. Group leaders from other colleges would come as guests. Long sittings, long discussions, hot and cold. The leaders would speak loudly, with anger, everyone would be reprimanded suddenly, and some would take offence. There was always fear of an attack by the Islamist party, and there was talk of confrontation. There was always a warning to be prepared and remain alert.

From one coffee house to the next, then from that one to a third. This is how the evening would pass, and then the night. I was new to all of it. Every day I would get some book to read and stay up all night reading it, understanding only parts of it. I caused my own bit of trouble, as I had not yet been included in the inner study circle of the group. My thing was about God. Is there a God or not? Every day I would stand up and half agree, and half disagree, with comrade Luqmani, a senior member of the group. But in the middle of the night, going home, I would become fearful. If there were a God, then what? That night Luqmani got angry, saying

"Haven't I already told you He doesn't exist? We have created Him. Our fear has created Him. All religions were invented just to rob people. There is neither sin nor virtue. The only reality is man, and nothing else. Read this book and come back tomorrow."

That night I lost heart. When I returned home, I vowed that I wouldn't talk to him next time—he didn't listen to me at all. It was a half Maghar night and drops of winter rain started falling. A gentle wind also blew. I walked along Lahore's Mall Road, and, turning at the public library, I felt as if I had been bitten by the tall trees there. The old, tall peepal trees along that road blew in my mind, and I shivered from the cold. Perhaps I hadn't eaten anything all day. My mouth was bitter from tea and cigarettes. The wind infused with the fragrance of the rain-soaked earth blew over the grounds of the Chishti High School, spreading in four directions.

I passed by the Laat Sahib, where the chief secretary used to sit in British times and the chief minister now sits, and crossed the Neeli Bar bus stop, named for that green and fertile region south of Lahore. I reached home and stood in front of the house.

It was crossing midnight. The rain had stopped, leaving the land drenched and making the coal tar roads shine like shivering mirrors in the blowing wind. Above, the clouds ran fast. Within them, the moon played like a child, peeking out occasionally by surprise. There was also a bit of warmth somewhere in the blanket of cold.

The usually alert houses of Krishan Nagar were silent today. The dim light of the moon made the shape of the standing houses more prominent. Otherwise, they couldn't be seen.

The last hurdle was how to get into the house. If I knocked at the door, everyone would wake up. Climbing the wall adjacent to the empty plot next to our building, creeping along the roof next to the rain gutter, and finally clambering down to open the window into my room, I was inside. I slowed my breathing to normal and then realized there was a sound at the doorway into the hall. It was as if someone had sighed or sobbed. I looked out of my room but couldn't see anything. I began to feel frightened, and I remembered Luqmani's words about God. "Oh God, have mercy!" I unconsciously prayed to God in my heart. "Oh God, forgive me! I won't listen to Luqmani." Slowly I put my foot in the doorway. There was total darkness, and everyone was sleeping, exhausted, in the other room. Suddenly my foot touched a body. She was lying on the floor, face down. Oh my God! It was the daughter of the family from Dubai.

The story of the woman from Dubai was very strange. The family had been living in Dubai for a long time, but they still had a house on our street. They had rented their house out, and then the renter and his family squatted in it, taking possession of it illegally, as happens so much of the time. A case was filed in court in an effort to force them out. After some years passed, the Dubai family won the case by bribing someone, but possession was another matter. Someone told them that as long as you don't come in person, you won't get possession. The men in the family all had jobs in Dubai, so the woman came back with the kids. But they still couldn't move into the house. The Dubai woman was actually from the old walled city centre, from a place called Rang Mahal. She would turn up every day and fight with the people in possession of the house, but they had gotten a stay of proceedings, so they refused to move. A few children would always come with her, with one of them trailing behind, whimpering, or stopping to play along the way.

She always had a troop of children with her, eight or maybe even ten. She was staying with relatives and would make a round each day on a rickshaw to come to the house. Sometimes she would visit with my mother, too. She was accepted as a part of the neighbourhood, and the whole *mohallah* seemed to be with her. If only the house were vacant, so that she could actually move into it. One day—God knows what stories she told to my mother—but she came to live with us with all her children. Maybe she was just hoping to put pressure on the renter. Without giving a second thought as to how everyone would all live in one room, my mother spread a cloth mat on the floor for the children. All day long there was wailing and crying, and bread was made and distributed. The children brought groceries from the bazaar all day long, back and forth. Our household would have otherwise been slowly dying of starvation, but that woman would just go to the bazaar to make a phone call, and the postman would come after a few days to deliver a money order.

My aunt fought a lot with mother about the arrangement, but once mother had consented, how could she refuse to let them stay? The woman from Dubai was tall and heavy-bodied, with skin a sheer black colour and a shining nose stud. She had attractive features, with a thin nose and large eyes. Standing with mother, she stared at my aunt, the veins in her forehead bulging, and said "Hoonh" loudly, at which point my aunt rushed inside, the tap-tap of her shoes echoing against the floor. With that, we finally reigned over the house, but it only lasted for a short time, a bit less than a month.

I remember that there was no water tap in the upper part of the house. There was only a small stove in the big room, for making roti. There was no proper place to wash dishes. On one side was a small stove, and we used to wash dishes near it in a tub. There was no drainpipe for the water we carried up from below, and so it would splash onto the rooftop and then run down the side of the house into a small drain in the street. A sewer system hadn't yet been built, and the streets were half finished and half unfinished. All day we would bring water in buckets from the ground floor, because of which the stairs were always wet. Sometimes a child would slip and get hurt. The woman from Dubai's eldest child was a daughter, and she beat her a lot. I don't know why. Her daughter was also sheer black in colour, and she was maybe a year or two younger than me. She was in her last year of school. But she lived in fear of her mother and worked all the time. So I never gave her much thought.

I was in college then. I had scored in the first division in tenth grade and so could proudly put on the uniform and go to the prep college. One of my other uncles paid for all the expenses, thinking I would one day become the big official that he had not been able to become. Instead, I became a new "revolutionary" and would look at my old friends in the *mohallah* as if to say, "Do you have no idea where the world is going? You are like frogs in a well, and you will remain that way." On top of that, I had my own separate small room, all to myself, and I told everyone that no one should show their face there. I didn't mind my own younger brothers so much, but I wanted to scare off all of the Dubai children. All day long I would wander around with my new college friends and come home late.

My foot touched the body lying on floor, and she sobbed a little with pain. I tried to look more closely at her face, but the Dubai woman's eldest daughter was stretched out, face flat on the floor. She didn't utter a single word, and I realized that her mother had beaten her severely, and, sobbing, she had fallen asleep here. This sort of thing had happened before, but I hadn't paid much attention. My mother always chastised the woman for beating her daughter so much. Her mother would say, "God knows where she has come from and how she got stuck to us! Does she look like my daughter? Neither her face nor her forehead. She's some jinn from the mountains. I wanted a boy so that he could help his father. I say, may she die today! I want to get rid of her, make her go away, far away,"

She did give birth to many boys afterwards. But what animosity she still felt towards her daughter! The girl was at work all day long, cooking, taking care of the younger children, washing their faces and bathing them, cleaning and dusting. If any work was left undone or anything got broken, her mother would beat fear into her. I felt really bad about this, but who could talk sense to that Dubai woman? She paid for our food from her own pocket, and that closed our mouths.

So I understood what had happened. I crouched down on floor near her and slowly passed my hand over her body. She sobbed a little with pain. A wave of fear passed through me, that someone might wake up. I leaned down to say quietly in her ear, "Did your mother beat you badly?" She didn't reply but caught my hand tightly. I continued to sit like that, on my tiptoes, and then pulled her slowly into my small room. She cried quietly, in pain. Without turning on the light in my room, I brought her to the mat on the floor of my room. A dim glow of the streetlights coming through the open window made it possible to see in the otherwise deep darkness of the room.

Outside, the sharp wind rose and fell. The cold increased and then relented, causing her to shiver. In the faint light coming from outside, I helped her to sit upright and looked at her face. She was still holding my hand tight, and the heat of her burning body reached into my body. It was the first time a girl had caught my hand like that. I was frightened, but the heat coming from her body also burned away my fear. She had cried for so long that her tears had dried, leaving bent, crooked lines across her face.

I caressed her face gently, and again some tears began to fall silently on her face. I don't know what happened to me that I put my lips on her tears and began to kiss her. She covered her face with shame. I lay down with her and held her tight, kissing her. She pushed me away at first and then finally relaxed her body. I asked her again and again, "How hard did your mother beat you? Where did she beat you? Where is the pain?" She put her hand over my mouth and asked me to be quiet. The wind struck the windows, and then it started to rain lightly. Rain in the middle of Maghar is seldom a downpour. There is just a splash of rain, breathing new life into the old season and causing the cold to increase yet further.

We lay like that for a long time, holding each other tightly. The heat seeping from our bodies was shared between us, breath by breath. If I tried to run my hand along her body, she would clutch it and hold it in place. In the darkness, I could not tell whether her pain had lessened or not. But she was at peace. Only later, after many more years of my life, did I come to understand that touch could bring such comfort to a person, could cleanse someone. I don't know when we fell asleep, or when I fell asleep. But her touch had made me forget everything, all the cares and exhaustion of the world.

The next day I slept late. I don't know at what point I closed my eyes, but when I opened them, she was no longer with me. The sun was shinning outside, but because of the night's rain, there was a touch of cold in the air. Never had my room felt so desolate before, my heart never so empty. It was the first time in my life someone had come so near to me, and then she had disappeared as if in a dream. A pang of yearning arose in my heart, and I wanted to cry. I didn't know when she had woken and left, so it must have been after I had fallen asleep. The daily routine was that I would get ready and go off to the college after getting a rupee or two from my mother, and then I would return late. I got ready slowly that day, taking a long bath, hoping that I might see her. But she didn't appear. Sometimes she would go to the bazaar with the other children to bring groceries. She'd be covered in perspiration and would quickly go to wash her face. At first I thought that I should ask her mother why she had beaten her daughter so hard, but then I realized that she would ask how I knew about it, since I always came home so late. So I kept quiet.

I never saw her again. A few days later, the Dubai woman paid a bribe to Ayda, and in this underhanded way she finally got her tenant out and was able to move in.

Ayda was notorious for getting things done for people for a price. He would never interfere in anybody's business unless somebody paid him to. Whenever I ran into the Dubai woman in the neighourhood, she would always invite me to her house, but I avoided it. The one or two times I did visit, I didn't see her daughter. Then suddenly she was married, and I don't know where she went. I got busy in politics and lost touch with the *mohallah*. After a few years, I left it altogether.

That night, like the half Maghar moon, continues to inspire me, at the edges of memories. That night has taken up residence on the silent walls of the empty nights of my life, blossoming and speaking inside my breath.

The Wall of Water

PARKASH DROPPED ME IN Amritsar from Jalandhar. The old man had come to meet me in Chandigarh. We reached Jalandhar by bus in the morning and then had lunch in his home; then he drove me to Amritsar in his son's car. I had a booking in the guest house at Guru Nanak Dev University in Amritsar. Although a bit distant from city, the university was beautiful. The guest house was even more so. It had large, spacious rooms, and mine was on the second floor, up a wooden staircase. I had arrived in India just after the Lohri festival, and it was winter. The rains chased us all the way from

Chandigarh to Amritsar. The old man had given me a meal, but he also told me that his wife didn't know I was from Lahore, otherwise she wouldn't have allowed me in the house, let alone offer me food. "She is firm believer in purity, and in caste," he told me. And then he gave me his trademark mischievous smile. Not only had I eaten lunch at his home, but I had wandered all through it. It never occurred to me to think of purity and pollution.

The old man dropped me off at the guest house in the afternoon. We'd had tea from a roadside eatery on our way. The old man didn't come up to my room, saying that he had to travel back as far as Jalandhar with his son. I was supposed to cross the border from Amritsar to Lahore after two or three days. Ten or twelve days had passed since I had arrived. I spent one week in Delhi and a few days in Chandigarh. I had come with some singers, but I was only a minor poet. Everything had just opened up. The chief minister of our side of the Punjab had recently visited East Punjab, and everywhere there were pictures of him side by side with the chief minister of East Punjab.

The old man went away, embracing me tightly. Emotions welled up in me. It was the third consecutive day we had spent together. He suddenly seemed to realize this, and he quickly dropped me off outside the garage next to the guest house gate and then disappeared in his car without so much as a wave of his hand.

He knew I was going to cry.

I wasn't particularly close to the old man. I didn't

really know him at all. We had met through a poet from London who was visiting Lahore. He was originally from Jalandhar but had been living in London for a long time. He shifted from a hotel to a friend's home the day after he arrived. We took good care of him and showed him around Lahore. This old man was a friend of his. I didn't have a visa to go to Jalandhar: Pakistanis get visas to India only for particular places, and that wasn't one of them. I rang the old man from Delhi. He said: "Don't worry, I'll come to Chandigarh. It is only two or three hours from Jalandhar. I'll stay with you, we'll wander around and meet some writers." The old man was a famous short story writer, but I didn't know about that. He wrote stories about forbidden relationships between men and women. There was a gap of about twenty-five years between us, but we became fast friends.

The day I came to India, I was on the verge of tears. I had come alone but was accompanied by all of my mother's stories about Batala, Peeran Bagh, and Gurdaspur. My father was from Batala, and my mother was originally from the village of Peeran Bagh, near the city of Gurdaspur. I had come primarily to see Gurdaspur and Batala for myself, but I also came for my mother, for all the memories and stories she had carried and given to me. I wanted to go to Batala the next day, but so far nothing had come together. I stood at the gate of the guest house, thinking. There was some open space outside the gate. Beyond it was a big garage, where a man was standing, watching me get out of the car.

It started drizzling. It was evening, and it appeared as if someone had laid green grass carefully over the earth. It was near the end of Magh, late in winter, when the sun appears only occasionally to give a breath of warm air as a promise of the coming month of Phaggan. The man quickly came towards me. He was tall, with a white moustache and beard, a tightly tied turban, and a neat and clean uniform. He appeared active and fit, but there were signs of his age in his movement. Evidently, he was the watchman for the guest house and, I learned later, also a retired soldier. I was frightened by the grave expression on his face and by his red eyes.

He greeted me with "Sat Sari Akal" and told me to go inside, to the front counter, and they would take my luggage up to my room. I didn't have much with me from Lahore, but I had collected a lot of books, some as gifts. I was puzzled by the layout of guest house. Why was there such a big gap between the gate and the garage? Leaving my luggage and making a dash to get out of the rain, I entered the guest house. There was nobody in the large entrance hall. As you came in, there were armchairs and some small tables near the door. To one side was a reception area, with a small room just off it. There was a man inside the room, and when he saw me through the glass, he came out immediately and called out my name. He also called out something about "Pakistan." It seemed to me that the guard out at the garage had overheard this and suddenly became wary.

The attendant then brought a key from his small room and gestured for me to follow him. We climbed the wooden stairs and stood in front of a door.

"This is your room, please keep the key with you. If you need anything, please let us know." I asked for tea, and then a phone. Mobile phones didn't exist at the time. "For the phone," he said, "you will have to come downstairs."

"Okay, I'll take tea downstairs." I spoke in Punjabi, and he replied in Hindi. He was from the east, from Bihar or eastern Uttar Pradesh. I had been listening to stories about people from that area coming to Punjab. "All Pakistanis speak Urdu," he complained, in response to my speaking in Punjabi.

I placed all my things where they belonged, washed my face and hands, and locked the door. I went downstairs. Night came out like a thief under the cover of the rain and threw a sheet of darkness over everything, hiding the world from view. A soft wind blew over the grass, as if treading with cautious steps. The dining room was closed, but some chairs and tables were placed near the door. The reception area was dark; only the small room attached to it was lit. I was standing in the area adjacent to reception, and I peered through the glass. The room was empty. I sat down on a sofa to wait, facing outside. The guard was sitting in the empty area next to the garage, and he stood up immediately when he noticed me. There was a wall of rain between him and me. There was light inside the garage, but the space between us was half lit and half in darkness. The rain itself seemed like a sheet of glass. On the other side of it, his eyes would appear at times, shining, and sometimes would blur away. The voice of the rain in the grass merged with the song of the air.

The attendant brought tea. I asked about the phone, and he gestured towards the counter outside the room with the glass wall, where the phone lay. Forgetting my tea, I called Harminder. I had met him in Lahore at a poetry gathering and then we saw each other again at a party. We exchanged phone numbers, and I told him that my parents were from the district of Gurdaspur and how much I longed to visit my family's ancestral place. He told me that he would facilitate my visit there whenever I came from Lahore. I had already informed him about my arrival from Chandigarh, and he was eager to meet up. He picked up the phone at once when I called and told me to get ready, he was on his way. What did I need to get ready? I made a few more calls and then sat waiting for him.

The rain became fierce, and the man standing outside by the garage looked soaked. He was hardly visible because of the torrent of rain. The dim light coming from the room seemed like stars in the rain, and the light was swimming, slipping, shining, secretive.

Batala is so near! They say it only takes an hour. One thing that my mother said had eaten me up: "Your maternal grandfather would say about my paternal uncles, 'You were seven brothers, and you all reached safety along with your families. I had only one son, and he . . .'" All of my paternal family had been in Batala. Mother had also come to Batala to live with her maternal aunt, who was my paternal grandmother as well. My maternal and paternal grandmothers were sisters. It was fortunate that my mother had come to Batala, because she was able to come across with everyone else. One of my uncles was a clerk in the Laat Sahib's office, in the Punjab Secretariat. My eldest uncle also had a good job. My father and two other uncles worked in the Electricity Department. The uncle who worked in Laat Sahib had brought all his brothers and their families on a rented truck with guards. But my maternal grandfather and one Mama, my maternal uncle, had stayed in my mother's village, Peeran Bagh, near Gurdaspur.

Mother was the last one left from her family. Her sister, brother, and parents had all died before, during or soon after Partition. Even her husband passed away when he was still young, leaving her alone with the little ones.

Harminder had still not arrived. I tried to extricate myself from the memories and stories and ordered another tea. The rain poured down. The remains of my paternal grandfather were in Batala, and I also had to visit the graveyard. My grandfather was quite well-off, but he was murdered in 1928. He had been appointed *patwari* of his original village, Qila Desa Singh, about sixteen miles from Batala. We had acres of land there, but the people who left my grandfather's dead body at our home in Batala early one morning said, "Do not try to come back to the village again." We were allotted a house of only fifty square yards in Krishan Nagar in Lahore after Partition; that included the allotments of both my mother and grandmother. My elder uncle was the wealthiest of all, and he was allocated a big house in Krishan Nagar, but he soon sold that house and built a big mansion on a quarter-acre plot in Gulbarg, a nicer area of Lahore.

The rain lessened around seven o'clock, but the wind was still strong and wet. At around quarter to eight, it stopped altogether. I recognized Harminder immediately. He was average height and wore thick glasses. He was wearing a short jacket and tie. "Oh," I realized. "He had to come on a scooter. That's why he had to wait until the rain stopped." Once he arrived, we left the guest house at once.

Sitting in the garage, the guard must have watched us go. But we were so happy to see one another that we were not aware of anything around us. Harminder talked nonstop, full of enthusiasm. In ten or fifteen minutes, he rushed through all the details of the plans for the next day.

I would have to reach the Golden Temple, in the centre of the city, on my own. He would meet me outside. Then we would have to do some shopping. "Amritsar's *vadian* snacks are famous. I want to buy some for you." I was preoccupied with how I was going to get to Batala the next evening. I didn't have a visa to go to Batala, so I would have to go there secretly, staying overnight and returning after visiting my parents' house in the morning. Harminder stopped once or twice on our way and came back with something wrapped in paper. "I'll tell you about it when we get to my place."

The first thing he unwrapped at home was chicken; he gave that to his wife. He told her that I had come from Lahore, and his son came to greet me with "Sat Sri Akal." Then he unwrapped a bottle. "I couldn't complete my service for you without whisky, could I?" he asked with a laugh. He leaned closer and said quietly: "I was once assaulted while coming home one night. I was on a scooter, drunk. They demanded my wallet. I was drunk, so I tried to fight them. I said: 'You motherfuckers, I am not giving you anything.' There were two of them. If there had only been one, I could have beaten him. They attacked me with a knife before they ran off, cutting my chest. I sat down, holding my chest, bleeding. Soon somebody passed by, and the police came. I survived somehow but remained in bed for many days. I still have the scars. But I had to stop drinking after that. My wife—you are my brother, so think of her as your sister-in-law—won't let me touch it. I got special permission today because of your visit."

Raising his glass, he said, "To your beautiful city of Lahore," and drank his glass in one gulp. Then, who knows how, but the bottle got finished while we kept talking. Then his wife came in and gave Harminder a long look. "It is almost midnight," she said, and then started serving dinner. "Just sleep here," he said. But I told him, "I have to be out tomorrow night, and it won't look good to be out two nights in a row. I hope to go to Batala tomorrow, and I don't have a visa. Please, would you drop me at the guest house?" His wife listened attentively. "No," she said. "Our son Jaswinder will drop you in the car. The rain is terrible."

While Jaswinder got the car out, Harminder gave me some books. I sat in the front seat with Jaswinder, and Harminder and his wife sat behind. "I wouldn't allow you to go alone," his wife said to me. "Who knows what might happen? Conditions are very bad here," she added. "I could have taken a taxi," I told her. "I've caused you so much trouble." She dismissed me. "Be quiet. What is all this crying about a taxi? How could we let you do that?" I kept my mouth shut after that.

There was some problem between Harminder and his wife, and they talked nonstop the whole way. By the time we reached the guest house, it was something like two in the morning. They dropped me at the garage and left straightaway. I ran to the big gate, fleeing the rain, and found it locked. I shuddered with sudden fear. I had forgotten to tell them that I would be coming back late. But there was a light on inside, and the guard opened the door slowly. He had a blanket over him and might have just gotten up from bed. I was still quite drunk. I looked at him and gave him a little smile, and then quickly climbed the stairs. For a moment, I heard the breath of someone running behind me. And then a thud of someone falling.

I hurried to get out of my clothes and fell into bed. I was drunk, so I fell asleep in an instant. I slept deeply, but had nightmares all night. People are banging at my door, yelling slogans. Then suddenly the door breaks open, and someone pushes my Mama and he falls on his elbows. Someone is on top of him. There is tumult everywhere. He puts up his hands to try to defend himself. He is struck by a sword, wielded by the guard at the guest house, with a tightly tied turban and red eyes.

I look around my room and notice that there appear to be drops of blood splattered on the wall. The rain continues, and the grave of my father is eroding. It is the lone grave in one of the open fields that belonged to my grandfather. "Now you have come to say your prayer for the dead," my Mama says. "You have come after sixty years to give me a shroud." Mother puts her hand on his face, she is wearing a suit the colour of henna. Mother once told me that when she arrived in Batala, she was wearing a henna-coloured suit.

I woke with a start, got up, and stood by the window. It was still dark, and there was no sign of dawn. I didn't know what time it was. There was a dim light at the garage. It is said that when Partition happened, it was during the monsoon, and it rained a lot. Everything was washed away in the water. Suddenly it appeared to me that the lawn of the guest house was soaked in red, and I could see the faces of the dead swimming in water there. I immediately backed away from the window and sat down on the bed.

My heart seemed to sink, as if I just couldn't bear it all. Oh my God, I am going to die here, I thought. I should never have come. The moment I crossed the border, my heart had begun palpitating, and it was as if I couldn't breathe. Was it because of my uncle's murder? I don't know. Just a kind of distrust started growing, and I had the feeling that I would die.

The sound of steady rain came in from outside. It had been drizzling all night. Finally, it was six in the morning; I had slept for barely four hours.

Sometimes the blood spilled by our own hands never dries. It courses through the coming generations, keeps flowing inside us for as long as we don't openly confront its source. And they didn't allow us to do that, to confess, to name that blood and what we did to each other. They do not allow us to meet. Otherwise, we could come together, sit and face one another, and ask, "Oh brother, why did you kill us?" Otherwise, we could go back to our lost places and find peace. Then people would say that whenever Punjabis meet, they talk and weep together. But when did you ever let us weep, when did you let us embrace each other? You could decide to move one place to another, perhaps, from here to there. But Amritsar will always be twenty-two miles from Lahore. You demolished the signs along the way, so that we would forget those living across the border. But where have they really gone, Lahore and Amritsar? They will be there, in the same place, as long as the world is here.

Now what has my generation done wrong? Why do our hearts remain soaked in this blood of the past? Whose hatred do we live with?

It is said that in everyone's life there comes a time when people look back and want to know where they came from. They remember their origins. This can happen at any time—in youth as well as in old age. Sometimes someone born in the next generation starts probing the past, grandchildren searching for the abandoned places of those who came before.

My grandfather had sprung up out of nowhere, like a mushroom. Almost fifty years had passed, and I had never thought about him. I had never seen a photograph of him, nor had I heard anything in particular about his life. When it finally occurred to me to ask about him, there was no one left to tell me. I didn't even remember anything about my own father, let alone my grandfather who'd been murdered in his village thirty years before my birth. But I did remember how my uncles would sit for long hours talking. And we children would sit by and fill the hookah bowl with tobacco. Mother used to say: "The women in the neighbourhood would say to grandmother, 'Dear sister, let your sons leave your house one by one, lest someone cast an evil eye upon them.'" My grandmother had seven sons. When my grandfather was murdered, my youngest uncle was just six months old. When my father died, my youngest brother was also six months old. All my uncles went at least as far as tenth grade in school. But my youngest uncle was the most successful. He became a judge. Having left the village after the murder, my grandmother took care of all her sons in Batala, all by herself, weaving cots and hair tassels for girls. She never accepted handouts. There was an amazing kind of self-respect in my grandmother that was inherited by all her sons.

Grandfather's story, though, did find its way down to our generation, at least through innuendo and rumour. It was said that our grandfather was a great drinker. That he kidnapped a Sikh girl from his ancestral village, Qila Desa Singh, and then couldn't ever return there. That he was murdered by Sikhs. And so it was: we were ruined in our own version of the scourge of 1947, which was already history when Partition happened. The elders knew the whole story, but our generation rarely spoke openly of it. Once, at a wedding party, one of my paternal cousins got drunk and accused all his uncles: "You are a bunch of cowards. Did anyone ever take revenge for grandfather's death? That is why grandmother lost her mind in her old age. They took all our land."

We were told only that our grandfather was great. There were horses and acres of land in that village. He was probably from the first batch of *patwaris* appointed by the British in 1915. When my elder, more religious, uncles would fight with my youngest uncle about his own drinking, he would reply through his stupor, "I am walking in my father's footsteps. You are the ones who have abandoned our father's ways."

One of my elder cousins told me, "A friend of your father used to live in Model Town, in Lahore. He was from Batala. He got all my uncles admitted to Batala schools. He would joke with my grandfather: "How it is that you have a son ready for school every year? Let our sister-in-law take a breath."

Now my grandfather has come alive for me. After one hundred years, he seems very close. Do bones wait for the living? People don't ever really die—they are just hidden from view. They live as remembrances in the house of the mind. People die only when they are wholly forgotten.

There was a knock at the door. The attendant had arrived to ask when I would have breakfast. I started. I looked at the clock and saw that it was already eight.

I bathed, got dressed, and went down to the dining hall. It was open now, and a few people were having breakfast. I ate mine quickly. I didn't see the guard from out front at the gate. Maybe he wasn't on duty this morning. I don't know why a wall of fear and doubt had risen between us. He must be a spy, I thought, keeping an eye on Pakistanis: whom have I been meeting? where have I been going? who is arriving to meet me? If I hadn't returned to the guest house last night, would he have reported on me?

There was no rain now, but the clouds were running wild. They appeared to be racing towards Lahore. It had been twelve or thirteen days since I had come, and I was feeling homesick. But knowing Lahore was so close was a comfort.

But then I remembered Batala. It was as close to me now as Lahore was.

Harminder had promised to meet me outside the Golden Temple. I went by auto rickshaw, and, passing through the streets along the way, I got lost in the magic of the people, shops, and places. Finally, I arrived at the Golden Temple grounds. I met up with Harminder, and we wrapped some cloth over our heads like caps, took off our shoes, and entered. There was a long queue to visit the interior of the gurdwara. I felt the place keep me moving, here and there, among the crowds. But I also felt a strange sense of calm and happiness, and I thought of the shrine of the Sufi saint Mian Mir, who was said to have laid the foundation stone of the Golden Temple. Even though I had never been here before, I had been to Mian Mir's shrine in Lahore many times. Whenever you visit his shrine, there is always a special quiet and contentment in the courtyard. The chirping songs of sparrows drift from the ancient trees surrounding the courtyard. But we always left quickly and did not linger to listen.

"You are leaving tomorrow," Harminder said. "Who knows when we'll have the chance to shop, so if you want to get anything, do it today." So I bought Kashmiri shawls, and he bought me the local snacks—*vadian* and *pappar*. Then he dropped me at an old book shop, promising he would come get me soon. The shop was originally in Lahore, and when the owner learned that I had come from there, he was thrilled. Though he had never himself seen Lahore, he felt that he had seen something of it, seeing me. He arranged for some food to be brought over from home, and we chatted without stopping. I didn't know where Harminder was; it was afternoon, and I was supposed to go to Batala today. At last he came back and drove me on his speeding scooter to the house of a professor, where he left me again. The professor told me that a friend of his was on his way from Batala and that he would escort me there. He was the manager of a bank, and he would take care of anything, so there was nothing to fear. "Harminder told me that you don't have a visa," he said. "Nothing to worry about. I visited my ancestral home in Sialkot without a visa. I was asked only to take off my turban when we crossed the bridge at the Ravi River. Now things are good. Your chief minister was just here. He was given such a grand reception that the queue of people lined up to welcome him was almost half a mile long."

We waited for some time. The professor had to attend a marriage party in Chandigarh, and he was in a hurry to leave. He finally received a phone call, and then he told me the bank manager had said that I should be dropped off at Punjab Club and that he would meet up with me there. Harminder took me to the club right away and told the people at the gate that I was the Sardar Sahib's guest. They had already been informed about my coming, and Harminder left as he had some work to do. He told me to phone him when I got back in the morning. The club was from an older time when everything was made of wood except the walls and roof. There were big open chairs and beautiful old tables. The cabinets at the bar were in the same old-fashioned style. A few people were sitting on stools, enjoying their drinks at the counter. It was quiet and very peaceful. Perhaps because it was evening, there weren't many people around.

The waiters invited me to sit on a vacant chair and asked me what I would like to have. "The Sardar Sahib will be arriving shortly," they told me. I said that I would prefer to wait for him. But they said, "We have been ordered to serve you. Please have something to eat or have something from the bar." The bar was full of foreign whiskies. I gestured towards one and took my seat with my glass. After a while the bank manager appeared and brought his hands together in greeting, apologizing for coming late. He was a gentleman through and through, probably about my age or a bit older.

He placed an order, and the waiter brought kebabs, tikkas, and some other dishes. He asked for his favourite whisky and raised his glass in a toast: "To your ancestral city, Lahore."

Then he said: "Partition destroyed us. Batala was a prominent industrial city. Batala Engineering Company was a big name. We heard that later its owner transformed it into the biggest company in Lahore. How could we have sent away such a diamond of a person? He was known as "Saabun" Sahib, because he started out selling soap on his bicycle. Batala is still where it was.

Amritsar is in the same place. But we have been locked away from each other. Lahore and Amritsar were once connected; now Amritsar is the last city of a new Punjab. Traffic has stopped; trade is finished. If the border were to open now, Amritsar would come back to life."

He talked without pause. Then he asked me to recite some of my poetry, and he recited some of his own, too. We discussed almost the whole world, and I drank a bit more. I wanted to forget Batala. Listening to him talk nonstop about Batala made me miserable. At last I gripped his hand and said, "Please don't talk about Batala. I can't bear it." It was my thirteenth day in India, and Batala had been walking beside me the entire time. We used to tease my mother by mentioning Batala.

His wife came around eight that evening. She had done a lot of shopping. Sardar Sahib said with a laugh, "Trips to Amritsar are very expensive."

His wife gave me a warm greeting and said with a sigh, "I know this grief. We are originally from Lyallpur, west of Lahore. My elders went to live there when the British gave out allotments in that area. We went to Lyallpur from Jalandhar and then came back again to Jalandhar fifty years later, having lost everything. We are Kahlon Jats. It wouldn't rain for many days in Lyallpur, and when rain did fall, it would instantly disappear into the earth." She spoke in one long breath, as if she finally had found someone to talk about these things with after so many years. But then Sardar Sahib indicated that she should be quiet and ordered dinner.

The drinking was having a bad effect on me. I was flooded by thoughts of my mother and Batala. It all seemed like a dream. I was going to Batala. For almost fifty years I had been listening to its stories from my mother and other elders. The Sardar Sahib saw that I had become quiet, and he understood. He seemed very wise to me. His wife seemed to like talking with me about Lyallpur and listening to me talk about Batala. I discovered a strange kind of connection with her. His own parents were actually from Batala. Indeed, the family was from the Ramgarhia community, which had settled in Batala even before the reign of Maharaja Ranjit Singh at the beginning of the nineteenth century.

It was already past ten by the time we ate dinner, and later still when we left the city. I couldn't see anything in the darkness. There was only the blackness of the road. I was lost in my drunkenness, which helped to hold back my tears.

They had me sit in front with the driver, and they both sat in back. Their car was quite roomy and fancy. The driver was attentive and had promptly opened the door for me. I sat silently the whole way, while they discussed their own things in the back. As we arrived in Batala, they told the driver to avoid the city. The market was already closed. Only some dim lights were visible here and there. It was like Krishan Nagar thirty years ago. Silent lanes, few people, and little movement. Most of the roads were dark, but shops were scattered here and there. Nothing seemed unfamiliar: it was as if I had seen it all before and then forgotten it, like some lingering fragrance in ancient places. A fragile light somehow burned in the darkness of my unconsciousness, like the shining eye of my mother.

They stopped at one point and gestured at an empty plot. This had been the home of Saabun Sahib, who owned the Batala Engineering Company. "C.M. Latif," I said. I had read his name outside a mansion opposite the Governor's House in Lahore. He was now the owner of PECO, one of the first steel factories in Pakistan. We sat there in the car for a while. I wanted to get out and kiss the road, but I stayed where I was. I had become very emotional, but I kept silent, slowly wiping my nose. He asked the driver to move on.

We soon reached their own home. It was like a small palace. A large house, a sprawling lawn, with a few cars parked outside. They took me into the drawing room, and then his wife showed me up to my room. I thought I would simply take off my clothes and go to sleep, but his wife had the servant bring me nightwear and slippers. I had just changed my clothes when an invitation arrived from Sardar Sahib. He was seated in a lounge-like room with a TV set. He had a bottle and glasses in front of him and was waiting for me. I was wonderstruck. "I had heard that Sardars could drink," I said, "but now I have seen it."

We had drunk so much at the club, but he wasn't finished. "Do you come here every day? What will happen tomorrow? If the border closes, no more meetings. Who can trust these governments?"

It was late. His wife was sitting nearby. It was quite cold and gas heaters were burning. The room was cozy and warm. The servants must have been ordered to arrange everything beforehand. Snacks were served: fresh fruit, dried fruits, and I don't know how many other things. I was not in a mood for any of it. Batala had made me sad. All my desire to come here had turned to grief.

Who knows, perhaps Sardar Sahib wanted to entertain me. In any case, he started asking about my family, about the murder of my Mama and all the others. But then he said, "You don't have the exact address, do you? Hard to say whether you will find the house or not. You can have a look around Batala, and I'll send two servants with you. They know the city. You can visit the main bazaar—but there is no graveyard." And so what of my grandfather's grave? I could not find my voice. "There is one shrine not far from the main bazaar, your mother must have told you about it. Even now they still light lamps in honour of the saint buried there. The city hasn't changed much: it has the same old neighbourhoods and streets. It's only when a house finally falls down that a new one is built. Only then do the maps need to be changed." I don't know how long he kept talking and drinking. Finally, his wife mentioned that it was time to get some rest.

I had nightmares about my grandfather and my Mama, my mother's brother, all night long.

The door is forced open, and someone kicks him. He falls on his elbows and tries to protect himself with his hands. Blood falls on the ground, falling and falling, and it is raining, raining. Meanwhile, the grave of my grandfather dissolves and slips away.

I woke up late in the morning. Sardar Sahib had already gone off to the bank. The maid was sweeping the floor. As soon as I opened my eyes, she went to call the Sardar's wife. She asked me whether I'd slept well and then told me to get ready for breakfast because the two people who would take me around Batala were already there.

I quickly took my bath, had breakfast, and went to the city. They had a scooter—only a scooter could go everywhere. I wanted to find my neighbourhood and the family home.

In the main bazaar, in front of a huge door to something like a fort, I saw two small turrets. On one side was a lion and, on the other, a horse, with a huge clock between the two. In the days just prior to her death, Mother said over and over again: "There is a horse on one side, and on the other a lion; there is a horse on one side, and on the other a lion." Today the secret of it was disclosed.

The family house was supposed to be located on the highest ground, up the hill. Once I was there, I had to find the brothers' courtyard, as it was called. The hill was there still, but the brothers' courtyard was gone. All the people nearby were new, among them a family of jewellers from Sialkot. When they found out that I was from Lahore and that I was looking for my ancestral home, they started to insist on giving me a meal. "You can't leave until we eat together. We won't let you go." At last I agreed to sit with them at a shop and have a cup of tea. There, one story flowed, and then more, words cascading like a flood. I just wanted to sit off to one side for a time.

I tried to send the people with me back, telling them to fetch me later. One said, "Sardar Sahib told me that we shouldn't leave you alone, that we should remain with you at all times. You don't have a visa for Batala." I remembered the guard at the guest house. He might have me apprehended even now, as I had been away all night. And then I started to think of other things. What is there in the relationship between these two countries that has anything to do with their people? Our governments have put all their energy into separating people from one another, not allowing them to visit their ancestral places. But then I thought, what will be, will be. Let me just see Batala: who knows when I will be able to come again? So I said to my companions, "Go and have some tea or something, and leave me on my own for a bit." They agreed, and I began to wander through the market.

My first thought was that I had been longing for this place for no reason. I wasn't born here, nor had I ever lived here; it was all new me. What is there here for me? My parents had ties here, and they were gone. That story was over. But then again, from my whole family, from among all my grandfather's seven sons and their children, I was the only one out of more than one hundred who had been able to visit the ancestral home. Is it the pull of the past? Why can't we forget our roots? Why do people want to return to them, again and again? Why aren't they just allowed to live, without this pull? And why are we forced to leave our lands in the first place? And then not return: is this some kind of punishment from the past that we have to endure? Were we ever given a choice?

Sometimes I think about my grandfather and try to add colour to the image I have of him. What shades do I use, after eighty or ninety years have passed? The graves have disappeared; there is no stone, no sign of them. For neither grandfather nor Mama. All that remains are the words and memories that mother shared with me all through her life. The thought of them intensified the pain of my separation from her. Memories of her infused my conscious and my unconscious with grief.

There is nothing for me in this city, I thought. It is just like all cities, nothing special. The only real place is the one where we live. Why do the shapes of these other places rise up in our dreams? Who is it, whose breath sends them floating through our minds in the white clothes of death, even as the grave is dissolving? Why do such nightmares return? Why do they devour us? Why doesn't 1947 ever come to an end?

Of all that was left here, it appeared nothing remained. My mother was only thirteen or fourteen years old when she left Peeran Bagh and Batala, and, having settled in Lahore, that is where she remained. She used to talk tirelessly, for hours and hours, about her ancestors. She spoke less about her mother and sister, and more about her father, who had come to Lahore by himself, and her dead brother.

I reached the green shrine. I thought it would be good to pray. The shrine was still in use, with fresh candles lit and new sheets laid out upon it. I kissed the grave and touched my forehead to it. The scent of incense filled the air. The voice of my mother rose up in me, and she was telling her story:

Our village was Peeran Bagh, a mile from Gurdaspur. When the land was divided, we left everything and came to Lahore. In our old village, we had a garden of mango trees. My father, Ghulam Farid, had his shop; mother's name was Zainab. There were ten, maybe twenty homes of Sikhs, ten or twenty of Christians, and ten or twenty of Muslims. Some people owned land. There were shrines to Sufi saints in the village, and there used to be an annual celebration for the saint, and a big festival as well. Qawaali singers used to come from Gurdaspur to perform:

Piran dia pira, sach dia piria
Purday kaaj dia pira
You the leader of all saints, you are the leader of truth.
You are the *pir* who encompasses everything.

My brother used to recite for the Prophet's birthday: "O God! That country is the most beautiful, where I have been searching for you from place to place."

We had a mare, a buffalo, and a cow, and about a quarter-acre of land. There were just two rooms in the house: one was used for animals, and the other for sleeping. My father was the imam at the local mosque, and at the time we left our home, he had gone to read the Eid prayer at another village called Khokhar. My one elder sister was married into the family of my maternal grandmother in Batala. I came to Batala one month before Partition. My father left me there, to go to Pakistan with them.

My older sister had already died. I was five years younger than my brother who was martyred.

It was announced that the attack would come on the third day. My brother led the Eid prayer in Peeran Bagh.

When Pakistan came into being, the Sikhs said, "Leave on the third day." There was one household of Shahs, descendants of the Prophet. They had given away acres of land to people. The Shahs said to my brother: "Please come to our home, the women are alone. We will bring a truck and a military guard from Gurdaspur."

When we fled our home, the hen had laid eggs; two chickens had been slaughtered and were ready to be cooked; the flour had been kneaded; the clothes had been put out to dry on the wall after washing. The milk was set to boil, and there was a sack of wheat in the kitchen. The greens had been picked and put to the side . . .

The Sikhs came and said to my brother: "You are the son of Ghulam Farid and we don't want to kill you. Run away." But when they came on third day, my brother was still there, at the Shah's house, because the women had been left there while the men had gone to Gurdaspur to bring the truck and the military. Maybe the Sikhs knew that the women were on their own, without protection. They warned: "Come out. If you don't, we'll cut through the roof." When the attack came, he faced them on his own.

He opened the door. One sword hit him on one side, and another on the other, and finally one hit his neck, and he was killed there in the courtyard. Everyone was forced out from hiding. They took the women and went away.

I saw it in a dream. They were slaughtering a camel. He was wearing a simple white tunic and a dhoti. That's what he always wore, even though he was a scholar of literature and learned in Arabic.

As they were taking away the women, they met the army convoy. The soldiers took back the women. My father was hiding in the home of a Christian, behind some sacks of cow fodder, and so he was saved. Then he came home and drank the milk. I had silver coins in a money box, but it was left behind. My father didn't bring any of the gold and jewellery that was hidden in the walls. He just brought two suits of clothes and nothing else. I don't know how he reached Lahore after locking the house. Then he left me on my own after just a few years, dead from the grief of the loss of his son.

Mian-ji, my maternal grandfather, taught the Qur'an Sharif to the whole neighbourhood. There was a huge banyan tree in front of our house. Girls would sit beneath it all day long, knitting and doing embroidery. There was a real sense of harmony. People came to the well, and the daughter of the Shahs would come with her spinning wheel. There were jujube, pomegranate, and mulberry trees all around.

And neem trees. My father was young and strong, like iron. He would bring the ground wheat on his horse, with two sacks on one side, and two sacks on the other.

FOLLOWING my mother's memories, I reached the end of the bazaar. It was time to turn back, and suddenly my heart and mind drained of everything. I started moving quickly, from the high point at the end of the market back towards the lower ground. I asked people about my home: "The brothers' courtyard, on the high ground." I got no information. I just kept wandering in the lanes. The houses were quite old. Some had debris in front of them. The walls along the paths were made of the old Nanak Shahi bricks, from the time of Ranjit Singh, with their fissures and gaps, through which the shy centuries peep. The lanes were the same as ever; only time had gone astray. The homes were the same, but their inhabitants had changed.

Closed rosewood doors had locks and chains. The softly carved wooden lattices on second-storey windows were falling apart. I reached the shrine.

The man who brought me was waiting. "I didn't find my home," I said. 'Shall we go?'

I didn't find it, but I did find something. "Rabb Rakkha —may God keep you" I said to my grandfather, 'Alam Deen, and Mama Hamid. I looked up and saw pieces of grey and white clouds moving quietly along in the blue sky, with the sun dodging in and out of their shadows. Phagun is the month when the sun and clouds play games of hide-and-seek.

I sat on the scooter.

Sardar-ji was waiting for me, and lunch was ready. I met a woman at their home. Amazing. She looked exactly like my elder sister, and when she said that she lived in Qila Desa Singh, I felt sad. The same features, frail and slim, and the very same voice. I talked with her for a long time. I was thrilled that she was from my grandfather's village, and I tried to forget that this was the same place where, some eighty years back, people had lifted my grandfather's dead body and brought it to the house of my grandmother, who later went mad. That woman from Qila Desa Singh: she wore a dark yellow shawl, and her hair was grey.

"I heard that you had come from Lahore to visit your ancestors' place, and I said that I would like to meet you." When I told her that our village was Qila Desa Singh, she kept insisting that I visit it with her, because it was not far from the place she lived. But at that point I wanted to go back to Amritsar. I might not have a visa for Batala, but I had seen it. That was enough.

After lunch, I returned to Amritsar by bus. It was just a forty-five-minute journey from Batala to Amritsar, and from there only half an hour to Lahore. Out of all my grandfather's seven sons, none was able to come back again. All of them died wishing more than anything to visit again.

It was evening by the time I returned to the guest house. Rain was coming yet again. In truth, I was afraid of the guard: he might call the police to find out where I had spent the night. Seeing me, he came right up and shook my hands with a "Sat Sari Akal." I was surprised that his hand was warm.

"Did you have a good visit to Batala? Did you see the places you wanted to see—did you find the home of your ancestors? You are fortunate to have had this opportunity." He spoke to me all in one breath. "Going back tomorrow?" he asked. "Yes, I'll go back in the morning," I said. He seemed to want to keep talking, but I climbed the stairs of the guest house. "He is acting friendly, but he is still trying to get information," I thought to myself. "He knows everything." I was sure that he was a spy. But maybe he wouldn't turn me in. Maybe, I kept thinking, I would get out safely tomorrow.

I fell onto the bed and immediately went to sleep. I was exhausted from the day. I had no idea how much time had passed when I was awoken by a loud banging on the door. The guest house attendant was standing outside. "Calls were coming all day long," he told me, "and you weren't around, and then you didn't come back at night. Now I've put the phone on hold, please come take the call." I splashed water on my face and came down to the phone. It was drizzling outside. Harminder was on the line. He said: "I can't come now. It is raining. And you are tired. We want to drop you at the border if you can stay just one day more." I told him that my visa would expire the day after next. "Whatever happens, I have to leave. Next time, for sure." I had no way of knowing that this would be our last meeting—that he would leave this world only a few years later in a road accident with his entire family.

It was nine at night. I must have slept for two or three hours. Now how would I get back to sleep? The servant served my meal. I ate sitting on a chair near the entrance to the guest house. There was a light drizzle of rain. I didn't see him anywhere. I had always seen him sitting in the garage or standing outside it, attentive, in his neat and clean uniform. There was a kind of furtive swagger in his manner. You couldn't really look at him, but you also couldn't ignore him. I had been afraid of him since the day I arrived.

I watched the rain fall in a steady stream as I ate my meal and drank my tea. How long would it rain? If it hadn't been raining, I would have gone out to a telephone booth to call home. Then I realized, perhaps it isn't possible to call Lahore. I would see in the morning. As I drank my tea, he appeared from somewhere, I'm not sure where. He reached out and took my hands, in a gesture of welcome, and held on for a long time. The warmth of his hands bored through the wall of my suspicion. He had removed his uniform and was dressed in normal clothes. "I took the day off today. I thought I would sit down with my friend from Lahore. I got some stuff for you. I know folks in Lahore call whisky 'stuff.'" Then he slapped a hand against mine and gave a loud shout of laughter that echoed through the whole hall. When the servant came to take the empty cup, I started to order another. But he waved the servant away. "Go up to your room," he said. "I will be there in a minute."

I really didn't want to drink with him. But what was I to do? I still didn't trust him. His show of open heartedness had created a crack in the wall of my doubt and mistrust, but the wall was still there. I kept on doubting him, fearing him. "He really isn't someone to fear," I told myself. But then, who knows? Maybe he wants to get me drunk and learn my secrets. Trapped in indecisiveness, I returned to my room. He immediately followed me, accompanied by the servant who was holding all sorts of snacks in his hands. "My dear friend, you have spent too much money," I began to say. But he cut me off.

"If you are from here," he said, "I am from there. My family home was in Badana village, in Lahore District not far west of the border. When the time came to leave, I was in the womb of my mother. I had three brothers and two sisters. Jawaala Singh—a general in Maharaja Ranjit Singh's army—was also from Badana. Some of my brothers became Muslims in order to hang onto their land; they are still living there. The others came here. My father sent us to Amritsar to live with my elder uncle, and he refused to leave his village, his home, not even at the last moment. He slept with the buffaloes. He kept saying, 'This is the land of my ancestors, why should I leave it?' We didn't even know where our village would be, this side of the border or other. Partition came so suddenly. People who had been living together for years became enemies. It was only when Partition happened that we found out our village was in Pakistan. It was attacked that very night."

He offered me his glass. "Cheers—to your Batala and my Badana," he said, and then emptied his glass in one gulp. His eyes were wet, and he grasped my hand. "Brother, I am a retired army man. This is the first time I have sat with a Punjabi from the other side. You are from my city. When the servant first announced that you were from Pakistan, my blood boiled. Someone like you killed my father and uncles. But why did anyone kill someone else? We were devoured by greed, eager to seize land and wealth, and we gave that greed the name of religion. When I found out that you're from Lahore, though, I wanted to meet you. Even so, my blood would grow hot again, at times. But now I am calm and at peace. I would love to see Lahore, and I could also visit my village, just as you have gone to Batala. You are fortunate." He told me that he had entered his village during the 1965 war between India and Pakistan and had seen his ancestral home. But he couldn't fire his gun towards Lahore, "How could I fire towards my own city?" he said.

We kept talking, on and on, for God knows how long. We shared our grief and exchanged phone numbers, but it was all in vain. It was not easy to come together and meet. He got drunk and kissed and embraced me and then fell asleep. I don't know what time it was. I had lost all sense.

The guard from the guest house—his name was Hardayal—woke me early in the morning. He brought down all my luggage, despite my insisting that he shouldn't. Harminder arrived at ten with his son. Outdoors, the sun was shining. The rain had stopped sometime in the night, but Phagun's chill breath of wind was still in the air. Hardayal embraced me tightly, "Okay then. Rabb Rakkha, Sat Sri Akal." His eyes glittered in the sunlight. I looked at them closely, and they were a kind of rosy colour. I thought for a moment that they might be red with anger, remembering all that he told me. But then I saw that the corners of his eyes were wet.

As I crossed the border, it seemed to me that a piece of sunshine was left in Hardayal's pocket, like the remembrance of his warm hands. I suddenly felt the cold of the passing winter. The terse behaviour of the staff at the border made the whole experience seem like a dream. And everything was contained in those dreams.

The dreams kept coming to me in Lahore, and I no longer knew whether they were of the streets of Krishan Nagar, Lahore, or Batala.

But there was one dream that I dreamt only after returning from Batala.

It is Batala's old bazaar. On one side there is a lion and, on the other side, a horse. A little girl, seven or eight years old, is wearing a henna-coloured suit. She is running towards the high ground, at the end of the market. Off to the side, my uncles and older uncles are all sitting together, wearing white cotton tunics and dhotis and smoking the hookah. I see the base and immediately recognize it. I used to heat up that hookah in childhood. Its silver water basin is shining. They are all sitting in a circle except for one man who is standing, his hand tucked into the cloth at his waist, and he is looking closely at the others with a half smile. It must be my grandfather. One can see it from how he stands. There are women and others around. Just for a moment, I see my grandmother and my elder sisters; their heads are covered, and they have tight ponytails.

Then they all vanish. The little girl running through the bazaar passes by me without looking towards me. Running on, she recedes into the distance, and then it appears that she has flown away and disappeared into the wind like a bird.